T0275527

© Maria Ródenas

POL GUASCH

NAPALM IN THE HEART

TRANSLATED FROM THE CATALAN
BY MARA FAYE LETHEM

Pol Guasch is the author of two collections of poetry and two novels. He holds a master's degree from King's College London and is a PhD candidate at the University of Barcelona. He has also been a writer-in-residence at the Santa Maddalena Foundation in Florence, Italy, and Art Omi in New York. *Napalm in the Heart*, his debut novel, has been translated into several languages. It won the 2021 Anagrama Novel Prize, making Guasch the youngest winner in the prize's history. He lives in Barcelona.

Mara Faye Lethem is a writer and literary translator from Catalan and Spanish who lives in Barcelona. She has translated novels by David Trueba, Albert Sánchez Piñol, Javier Calvo, and Patricio Pron, among others.

NAPALM IN THE HEART

NAPALM IN THE HEART

A NOVEL

POL GUASCH

TRANSLATED FROM THE CATALAN
BY MARA FAYE LETHEM

FSG Originals

FARRAR, STRAUS AND GIROUX

NEW YORK

FSG Originals
Farrar, Straus and Giroux
120 Broadway, New York 10271

Grateful acknowledgment is made for permission to reprint the following
material:
Extract from *Bihotz Handiegia* by Eider Rodríguez. Copyright © 2017 by
Susa. Used by permission of Salmaia Literary Agency.
Extract from "Hell Is Where We're Bound." Copyright © Marina Tsvetaeva,
1915.
Extract from "Phantasia for Elvira Shatayev," from *The Dream of a Common
Language: Poems 1974–1977* by Adrienne Rich. Copyright © 1978 by
W. W. Norton & Company, Inc. Used by permission of W. W. Norton &
Company, Inc.

Library of Congress Control Number: 2024937056
ISBN: 978-0-374-61295-5

Our books may be purchased in bulk for promotional, educational, or
business use. Please contact your local bookseller or the Macmillan Corporate
and Premium Sales Department at 1-800-221-7945, extension 5442, or by
email at MacmillanSpecialMarkets@macmillan.com.

www.fsgbooks.com
Follow us on social media at @fsgoriginals and @fsgbooks

10 9 8 7 6 5 4 3 2 1

NAPALM IN THE HEART

BURIAL

The cold came as it always does. Look: one morning you wake up and the ground is white. The days were short and frozen. From the window, things seemed small and insignificant. If the snow lasted a week, it was here to stay. And that was already the case: the first autumn rains hammering down onto the dry ground, turning the roads into swamps and cutting us off from the city; the dampness that dissolved into a sudden dryness; and the snow that marked the beginning of an era whose end we couldn't foresee. From the window, the trees appeared just as close, just as far away. When the air grew bold, it broke the frozen twigs and the few leaves that were still attached. Foxes came down from the forest and roamed empty houses. Hot-blooded animals in the cold. Because they knew we would give them food. I watched Vita, how she came out onto her porch and left them chicken bones and skin on a plate. They crept closer, growling and baring their teeth at each other. The ones that didn't get anything at Vita's came over here and waited at our door. I put out stale bread dipped in milk. They devoured it.

I

The realm of silence, I said, when will you return from the realm of silence?

EIDER RODRÍGUEZ

EXHUMATION

Snow melted on the land that throbbed like a hot marble surface; dirty puddles boiled. The first dahlia leaves sprouted up and time swept away the last frozen piles gathered along paths and roads. There was a tree, a very tall one, that sent out tender shoots where aphids circled greedily, slurping its sap. Every day was a well of life illuminated from the depths: we closed our eyes so we could see, and greeted each other from the windows, hiding our bodies behind the curtains. We could only see each other's hands and, on rare occasions, glimpse the derelict gardens. A layer of phosphorescent pollen accumulated on the cracked paving; it looked like the powder left on corners to scare off dogs. Everyone had a hive in the bushes by their front doors, solid and dripping with propolis. Starlings and robins came and devoured the bees, chirping, and took their honeyed beaks back to their babies calling from the trees. Peace was not a feeling, it was a place: the grass that already reached our knees; the animals racing by, seen by us as mere movement sketched amid the brush. Creatures that came from the forest and walked along the fractured road and nursed their young on our porches. I read somewhere that wolves had been seen in packs, striding among the houses. Boris later told me: 'I saw enormous wolves coming down the hill.' It was in the first letter he sent me.

I whispered to myself, repeatedly,
'Day nine hundred':

Boris, dear Boris,

The man with the shaved head is at our house again. I was coming in from the vegetable plot and found him sitting at the table. And I thought I saw Mother beside him, small, as if his arrival had shrunk her. On the table there was toast and tea. I looked up: they were smiling with tightly pressed lips. I went up to my room without a word. I couldn't look him in the face: they spoke the other language. Mother's eyes narrowed as that man told her fabricated stories. But she truly believed them and kept nodding her head, taking small bites of toast, nodding yes oh yes with her forehead, listening to his lies and swallowing it all. A bite of this side, then a bite of that corner, now another sip to make another lie go down. What the fuck could she possibly understand, Boris, when she never speaks that other language, when I've never seen her speaking it ever?

This is the third day he's come. The first time, he was delivering Vita's pension, but said he'd knocked on our door instead, by mistake. At first, Mother looked at him warily and only partially opened the door as she spoke to him. She stuck her head out into the shaft of light. But they chatted for a long time and I could only understand some of their words. When he turned up again, with no excuse that second time, they strolled through the garden: Mother showed him the vegetable plot and the hens, the cow and the rusty gate that leads to the forest. She laughed as she pointed out the trees and the plants and the hill, and he nodded to her words. Today is his third visit. Now it's Mother who is the one constantly nodding.

I don't like him, Boris. He has eyes like an animal. And he walks like an animal. And he smells like an animal. I hate arrogant eyes like his, I hate lying tongues, those that rush towards evil and make brothers fight each other. I hate them. And his head is shaved, like all of them. That is what they're told to do, and they do it. They only know how to follow orders and then they go around bossing other people about, and telling them what they should and shouldn't do, because they never talk back to the people ordering them around. They don't dare. But you know that already, Boris, you know how they bark orders, pointing their machine guns. I'm sure the ones who did that to your parents were just the same, Boris, I'm sure of it. Dead sure.

I should leave. Life here goes on with the same old rhythm. It's never slow, but it's a cold, cold coldness, like the world is still frozen. I think of you and from my mother's window I look out at the rat room. When I miss you, I go back there: to the rat room, our room. Sometimes I'm scared we'll never see each other again, scared I risk never being happy with you again, and I need to be in that room. I love you the way we love those who've left long ago and those who haven't yet arrived, those we've never seen or who've never yet existed: Boris, you.

Yours.

P.S. Also, Boris, my granddad died today.

SIGN

There was so much phosphorescent light that morning that we found circles of fish floating in the water and flocks of birds on the ground, gathered one last time to die together. First there was an incredibly loud bang, the light that emerged from the Factory veiling the sky for hours and then, silence. An implacable, opaque silence. Those of us who didn't leave remained inside at home, bored to death, counting wooden beams and filling the little wormholes with pins. Boris and I started writing to each other. A few tanks stayed behind, and some soldiers who brought the old ladies their pensions and delivered our letters. Drunkenly, destroying the rooms, breaking the windowpanes – they also cleared out the houses of those who'd fled. They would often drag one of the remaining women into a house and she would emerge hours later with her face battered. They spoke the language they wanted us to speak, but we refused. When Vita came back, with her sister, some months later, she found her graves covered with green foxtail. The first thing she did was wrench it all out and then lie down on the smallest grave, clawing at the earth. I felt sorry for those ugly plants that'd taken root there, since the other kids always taunted me, chanting: 'Scrubweed, scrubweed,' and I had been watching that foxtail grow slowly, a small unruly forest sprouting up in a tidy garden.

I found him dead among the tomato plants, and cold, cold as the morning frost. I mistook his wrist for a cane stalk, that's how thin it was. And his expression was tranquil, as if he had died repeating to himself that he'd seen enough of the world, and that he was leaving in peace, returning to one of the tasks he had done the most during his life, which was growing and caring for plants, so that he could later gather their fruits. His large ears, like bristly leaves: the pointy white hairs on the lobe, travelling up the cartilage. His dark skin, dried out by the sun. Grandpa, dead: his heart destroyed. From so much waiting. Broken, from so much beating. For nine hundred nights, he'd held out. Nine hundred identical mornings. I didn't cry. When I realised that his wrists were not hunks of cane, I also recognised the hands that had drawn a cross on the head of one of our puppies: the litter had just been born, seven little dogs and you could fit them into your hand two by two. While I was playing with a white one with black splotches around its eyes, saying, 'You're mine, little guy, all mine,' it fell from my hands to the ground, poor little thing, and shrieked with a high-pitched death rattle I'd never heard before, as if someone had pierced its throat with a needle. But Granddad picked it up while it was still breathing, and nursed it for weeks until it was better and could reunite with the other puppies. Before he put it back he dipped his fingers into a blood-coloured paste he kept in a jar and traced a red cross on its forehead. We wanted to keep one of the litter, before giving them away, but not the one who'd fallen, who might turn out badly, Granddad told me. 'The only good dogs are guard dogs, strong dogs.' He was holding it in his hand while he said that. I saw Grandpa's withered wrist as if at the same time a part of the old world was dying too, reddish, the world of hoes and dusty dirt, that was now kilometres away, quite distant, and I hardly had words to describe it. Like I was watching a film with a veil of frost over my eyes.

MOON

In the first letters that Boris wrote to me, he told me that he took photographs because he didn't have the words to explain what he believed was happening. He developed and printed them in the apartment in the city where he lived, in a darkroom that his father had built. His parents have been gone for a long time. He keeps a wrinkled portrait of them, carrying it in his pocket wherever he goes. He says that he takes photos to get closer to what the camera freezes in time. To show things that happen. To turn experiences into truth. But also because photographs have a crepuscular aura, and there's something crepuscular and elegiac about Boris too. Every time he takes a picture he confirms that time is passing and he feels very important, in every way, because he is taking part in the death of that tree, by depicting it, and that cat, and the faces of his parents, and that's how he explains it. And photography is a perfect fit for Boris, with that eclipse always in his eyes. Always half absent, like a photo, lurking on the cusp of another reality. Anaesthetising. Omnipresent.

When the man with the shaved head leaves, I tell my mother: 'Grandpa's dead, in the garden.' We don't know what to do with him. My mum says let's throw him into the river, but Vita says no, that the river's not strong enough, that it's just a tributary of the Tet and wouldn't carry a corpse, that Grandpa would linger in the shallows for days, animals would come and we'd have to watch them fill their bellies with him. And since we don't have the time to dig a deep hole, because the flesh on old bodies is more ripe for death and rots in just two nights, Vita says we should chop him up and bury him in the garden, to feed the soil, that Our Lord would understand and not hold it against us. I didn't think she was serious, but when my mother looks at me with those bullet eyes of hers I obey, unable to stop wondering if she's angry with me or what I've done to hurt her. As I run the saw through his frail wrists, images cycle through my mind: when we dug the pond together, I with a little pail and he with the large shovel and wheelbarrow, carrying the dirt into the forest – now his ulna and radius are putting up a fight – when he would tell me about his father, returning from the war with his body full of shrapnel, stubbornly silent until the day he died, not opening his mouth even once – now his neck vertebrae and his spurting aorta – about when his brother was being born and from the garden he could hear his mother's screams and then the neighbour lady came, bovine and cold-blooded, and told him they were going to die, and my grandpa, poor thing, didn't stop crying over the sixteen hours of labour, thinking that his mother and the baby would slowly disappear – now his thin calf, like chicken flesh, and the thick fibula, that screeches as the blade hits it.

CRUSADE

I loathed being bound to others not out of free will, but by their slimy, viscous hatred. The animal eyes, the rocks, the gashes. Their imposition: that I embody an idea they've thrust upon me. Their undoing of me, first, and then undoing my illusory world, and then their remaking of me in ordinary flesh that they find acceptable: muscular, tautly tensed, animal. My body mutated under others' gazes: it shrank, it expanded, it burst. My body sunk into a world it wasn't built for. I lowered my tone. I spoke in a mumble. And I got used to speaking in such a soft voice that only those who listened attentively could even hear me. Boris was the only one who could. In fact, he preferred silence. When my mother told me that she knew about us, concealing her rage at the entire world in the bulging vein on her neck, she said quickly: 'I don't care, I won't tell anyone, I'll keep your secret.' I responded that when we say we don't care about something it's because we really do care; otherwise, we wouldn't say that, and we'd just carry on, the same as ever. That was how the memory often came back to me, of the first time my mother saw Boris, as if in that exact moment she discovered who I was.

My mother and I, and Vita now watching from her window. A thin wispy fog and clouds stained by the bleeding moon. 'You've been good,' Mother says, as I distribute the small shreds of flesh and splintered bones amid the furrows. I place a fragment beneath each plant, so they will grow hardy. Poor Grandpa was so fearful that he would've wanted to be buried deep, the further from us the better – the more alone inside a fibreboard box, the better. And he, who'd been so scared as a boy that he whistled on his walk home so everyone would hear him, must now turn over in bits, there in that soil amid earwigs and earthworms. He will nourish them. And he will make them grow and raise thousands of miniscule eggs among the stones. And identical copies will be born, but even smaller. And he will become one of them. And then we will fumigate the garden with garlic oils, killing him again, one more time. No rest for the poor man. Chopped in pieces and buried in pieces. I took after my dad in everything – including his walking so close to madness that it burned – but not his wide, tall body; in that I was more like my grandpa; a slender little slip of a thing.

DESIRE

When Boris talked to me about a country to live in, I always reminded myself that he was profoundly nostalgic, deep down, because he was missing something he'd never had, and that's the worst nostalgia you can have. When he would talk about it at the end of the school day with the other boys it was as if they shared only an anger, nothing more – that they were linked by that anger, bound together by that anger – and I saw their veins thicken like garden hoses filled with pressurised water. I didn't recognise him and wondered: what are you saying, Boris? When he talked with a deeper voice, as if speaking in public or in front of his parents. And he seemed fragile, he who's so cocky, talking about the past with his head in the future, two times that don't exist. Where are you, Boris? With the boys, who together would shout: 'Rage, rage against the dying of the light!' They must've read that somewhere, they couldn't have made that up themselves, but they didn't explain it. They just repeated the phrase, louder and louder each time. 'Rage, rage, rage!' And they also said: 'Look how a tiny flame lights up a huge forest. And the tongue is a flame!' And when I get bogged down in those memories, when I remember the days Boris and the other boys went through the streets repeating that, I feel a little sorry for myself. Because I remember being by his side, with them, mocking the other language, which we did in secret because ours was the little one, the absurd one, the insignificant one; mocking the other boys' pronunciation, their inability to understand our world, and I remember how I joined in with all the different ways of laughing they had. And I see myself there now, from a distance, and I see that I only did it to feel a little closer to them, just a little, and to forget, for a while, about the other things that I had to shoulder, the things I hid in the silences.

From the window I locate the garden furrows with their unexpected fertiliser. As if the earth were blacker. A bit more dead. And the tomato plants a bit more alive, more taut, thicker. As is happening to me right now: sometimes I think I'm annotating the future. I tell myself that even when I don't understand, I still have words. Someone, perhaps, will be able to understand them. Somehow, I decide to keep what remains. And when I tire and want to go outside, Mother comes and tells me: 'Don't go out.' She only leaves me the keys once in a while, to help her or to go see what they're doing at Vita's house, spying from afar. But Mother always goes out, and repeats: 'Nothing can happen to me. I'm old.' I go out too, she doesn't see me, and I take the paths that begin at the end of the bramble patches and I head into the forest. And I know that she knows I go out, that I manage to, that I go up and I go down, but she always insists on the facade of things and on the lies that, from saying them so many times, become truth. She also often tells me: 'Now, the Earth . . .' she grows silent for a moment and then continues, 'has shrunk. We've lost our sense of eternity. We no longer know where we are.' And I listen to her, and it saddens me to see her that way, as if bleeding, when she says that. She also responds, when I tell her about Boris: 'Anyone who only loves one single thing doesn't love anything.' And she reproaches me for that because I must talk about him as the start of it all. She sleeps with elderflower on her bedside table, she wakes up with the light of the newborn day and she comes down the stairs, counting, and before going to bed she says: 'I've climbed so many steps,' and she writes them down in a notebook where she records her ascending and descending each day. But then she says that it doesn't matter, not to her, what's going on, and she won't waste the years to come watching as the fruit rots on the ground where it fell, cracked open. And meanwhile, she looks at the stars, at the sky, and she pours out everything that needs to happen, and her hopes too. She memorises the rotations of the stars, the coincidences of the satellites, the phases of the moon. To forget about the others, obviously, as if she lived alone, but most of all to forget about herself.

I whispered to myself, repeatedly,
'Day nine hundred and three':

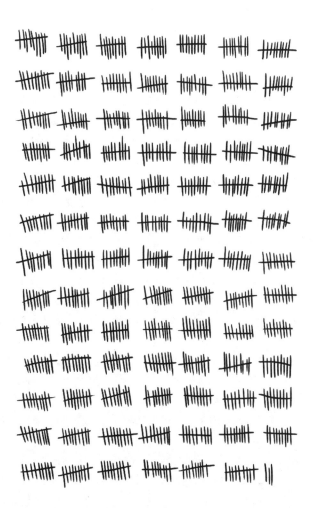

Forgive me, Boris, forgive me.

I swear I didn't want to hurt you. I was enraged because he was right below me, in the kitchen, talking to my mother, as I was writing to you. His scent climbed the stairs and stuck in my throat. And that was why I told you that they must've been like that, the ones who did that to your parents. But I don't know, obviously; you're right, obviously I don't know. He'd placed his hat on the table, but was still gripping it in his hands. I looked at him and thought: You can't put down your shitty hat for even a second, lest we forget that we've allowed the wolf inside. And when I went up to my room, my body was trembling – my legs and my arms – because I couldn't believe that we'd let one into the house. And now I remember when my mother told me 'hide and don't come out', pointing to the trunk, the first time the men with the shaved heads came. And the weeks have passed, and with the weeks, the months, and the years, and today only one of my legs would fit in there. Now they are inside. Now they know that my mother isn't alone, that I exist, and that I'm not a small child. And now what, Boris? Now, what?

I slept for a little while and dreamt of you. You came to the forest and we were together. The sky was long, soiled and clotted, the colour of aubergine; there was also a light like green flesh traversing parts of the air, and ancient music – just a slim echo of some obscure voice. Later, we were on beaches that stretched on for kilometres, swallowed up by some immense force. And we were there in the middle, in the sea. Unlike other dreams, this one was serene, and it led me painlessly to waking: I loved you there in that dream in a way I'd only thought about loving in life, and that was long ago, even before I knew the names of things. Suddenly, we vanished from the sea and the horizon was water. All water.

When I awoke, that man came into my mind and I felt anguish. To get some air, I went up to the hill, and from there I saw the city: what a desert of skyscrapers! I imagined you in one of those buildings, but it had been so long since I'd gone there that I couldn't say which one was yours. Back at home, I keep moving like before, but with an uneasiness in my chest I can't shake off because in every moment I'm thinking about my dad, and about my granddad, about life before this, about you, about the things you tell me that I don't understand, and which now grow larger, immense, and I understand them even less, covered as they are by the snow of an implacable winter, but even when the sun comes out and the flowers bloom, and the snow melts, I don't understand anything, Boris. I still don't understand a thing.

DIGESTION

Before dying, life was everywhere – fish migrating upriver, against the current; the end of the bear's hibernation, its bellows echoing through the valley; the bees about to explode like bullets from so much pollen – life was being born everywhere. Suddenly night fell on us, a clear and shining night that covered the houses where we lived with a giant glass bubble, and the forest too, and even the city beyond the hill, and inside the bubble the light multiplied until it was blinding. Who would lift it up? They had razed the curve of the hill on the other side, the side we couldn't see from our home, and they'd dug pits into it, deep as a throat, where they threw the dead. Some men dressed in white from head to toe kept tossing bodies in there, more and more dead. And some poles, beside the pits, held flags that must have been as big as our house: hundreds of identical flags. I had gone up there with my mother, hiding behind trees, and I hadn't returned to the top of the little hill since. The immense city, on the other side, and half the hill bald and open like a black hole that was gradually swallowing up the landscape. Mother and I, freezing, saw how people were piled up inside there, but there were also trees – rickety and ill, dry and red – and clothes and food, and a lot of earth. They threw earth into the earth. And later we found out that they threw men in there because they'd banned burials, that the neighbours by the cemetery had put up barricades at the gates, set fire to them and said that those dead bodies, that had died of who knows what, could not come in.

26

First thing in the morning. The sky weighs heavily on our roof. I imagine a whale shifting on the tiles and the space separating my chest from its belly vanishes. Now the whale is on top of me. Its ocean is between my nipples. I get up. I leap over the gate at the back of the garden, which is so rusty that the bolt won't open. I don't take anything with me, just the clothes on my back and the little jack knife, because it was a gift from my dad and I carry it with me always, squeezing it tightly in my fingers when I go out, so I'll feel less afraid. My mum told me many times that someday she'd explain what was going on in the forest, when I was older and could understand it. She never did explain. I'm so focused on the path that a sudden movement amid the leaves makes me lift my knife and point it at the sky, as if defending myself from someone I can't identify. There is an owl, looking me up and down. I see myself through its eyes: so useless and innocent, aiming my knife at some god, and I close my eyes against the shame that fills me. Like when, as a boy, I would arrive home in the afternoons to my tired mother and cry out to her: 'Mummy, the shame,' and she would respond: 'My son . . .' and I would look at her, waiting for her to continue, 'you'll always feel it, and you will only be able to live with it if you learn how to make them feel ashamed, when they see you proudly bringing that shame to life, when they see you living with it like you would with a third arm or a third leg or a third eye.' The whale between my nipples: its ocean.

BIRTH

In the real world, something happened and I didn't know what it was. I always wanted to know what was happening, and my mother would warn me that I'd go blind if I spent too much time searching for answers, for god up there in the sky; because she didn't know how to simply tell me I was curious when I asked her questions. I could never get enough, and I always wanted more. Here, in the real world, something will happen and I don't know what it will be. And I always want to know and I don't know, and Dad would tell me, as he caressed a rope, that we have to always pay attention, because the future gives us clues, and we just have to know how to read them. And if I think about Boris's universe, the one he freezes in those images, something's already happened, and it will always be that way. No one will ever be able to change it. Maybe that's the reason why he takes so many photos and he's always going around everywhere with his camera storing up the world, and in his pocket he always carries a portrait of his parents when they were young, because there they will never grow old.

With my jack knife in the air, like a hero from an ancient myth pursued by the pathos that leads him to an unremarkable end, I find myself in the forest. The silence sleeps inside me and the vastness calms me down. Where does this drowsiness come from? The world is immense, grandiose, with dark and wrinkled fruits hanging from the trees and mosquitoes the size of walnuts orbiting my legs. The damage to the world has already been done. The words have congealed inside my head. The rocks splattered with rotted, treacly flowers that dry up like fossils on the surface. My heart beats in my eyes. The tingling, in my hands. And I see the eyes of the beasts hiding behind the bushes. A restless darkness and hundreds of glowing dots bespangle the ferns. The rawness of the universe is tranquil – the animals listen to me, and I listen to them.

GAZE

The muteness of the dead, the presence of the dead and the indictment of the dead sent shivers up my spine. It was always that way. I passed it every morning, on my way to school, when I took the road that led to the city, and also in the afternoons, when I returned home. I always went past there because the shortcuts through the forest still frightened me. His bust observed me with a cold gaze, reproaching me for my inability to stand erect like him, such a man, with those arms and that rigid back, those fixed eyes, and that finger pointing forward. I didn't know who he was. I lowered my head as I passed, believing that would keep me safe. Enormous. The height of a tree, two trees. Like a golden god. It was always warmer in front of him because the light reflected off him, often blinding, and melted the snow that carpeted his feet; and in the summer it was hell, burning so hot we all avoided passing near. The same face as in the photo my parents had hanging in the dining room. Small enough that we didn't have to look into his eyes; big enough that we couldn't forget he was always there. For me he had no name. I never remembered what it said on the plaque. And I always forgot what he looked like. If I thought of a man's face, it was the face of the men I saw working, coming home, moving through the house, leaving the house and returning there later. My father's, my grandfather's. They knocked it down as if they were doing something forbidden, while in the background noisy trucks were forcing people out. A lot of ropes and a lot of men. And when it fell, it didn't break, but they left it there, lying on the ground, blocking the road from one end to the other. Like trees when they fall, that lie there where they've fallen.

When I reach the top of the hill I imagine I am seeing myself from my window, that the long dot on the peak of that little hill would be me, up there. But what I couldn't have imagined, from my bed, was what I could now see, into the other valley: not our few houses, no; a city that throbs in its sleep, clouds that flame up and a permanent silence emptied of life. As if I were holding my breath and, at any moment, could start breathing normally again – if those who bring the city to life just came back, retracing their steps to each house and lighting the fireplaces, and if smoke came out of the chimneys and someone bothered to trim the bushes out by the door, if they polished the splintered wood and changed the curtains, repaired the panes and washed them to gleaming again. On one side there are those few old homes that needed repainting, surrounded by green and the life hiding beneath the branches; on the other, a presence that rises among the skyscrapers and the glimmering glass walls, mirroring each other: an empty kaleidoscope; and also the back of the hill, stripped, with the covered pits, and a desert of people who've never met each other.

LOVE

When my dad was alive, we started keeping chickens. I would give them names. One was called Pector. I can't remember the others, because I grew up and stopped naming them. I cried the first time I came home to find that one of the hens had disappeared. 'When we eat animals,' my mother said, 'we become more like them. You are the only one of us who won't take on Pector's face.' I looked at myself in the mirror and smiled: I loved them in silence, from a distance. I would wash them every other day, gather up the feathers they lost and store them in a box, and I would file their beaks so they didn't break their skin when they scratched themselves. Clarice was the last hen I loved: when she appeared on our table, I wasn't hungry but I devoured her, praying. With each bite, I felt her that little bit closer to me. Oh, Lord, that was a true homecoming! I would look into my dad's eyes, as he picked up the thighs with his fingers and ran his tongue over the roasted skin, and I would feel a torrent of jealousy rising up from my belly, against the bile: I wanted her all for myself. The years passed and my mother would tell me that all I had of Clarice was her voice, so shrill. And the way I constantly flapped my hands and arms, as if they were wings. And also her gaze, suspicious of everything.

On the way home, returning from seeing the city, I don't understand where all that life has ended up. And I am even more confounded thinking about this life, mine. This house. This mother. This forest. Boris. These letters. These pigs. These days. This world, rotting from all its tranquillity. A fox follows me, agile, and I sit down on a log by the side of the river, worn smooth by all the men and women who'd sat on it. I begin to list ideas I'd never thought of before. One, that I don't feel I've ever been a boy, and I don't really know why. Two, that I resemble my dad more and more. Three, that it's been a while since I've prayed not to end up like he did. Four, that if we don't repaint the wood, the house will collapse in a couple of years. The walls, the ceiling, the corrugated roofing sheets for doors, the bundles of reeds that act as buttresses. All to the ground. Of those ideas, I'm most worried about the fourth. And I keep thinking of other things, slightly afraid of the fox, because it is the first time I've seen one up that close, and I don't know if it's still there with me or if it has already departed.

I whispered to myself, repeatedly,
'Day nine hundred and five':

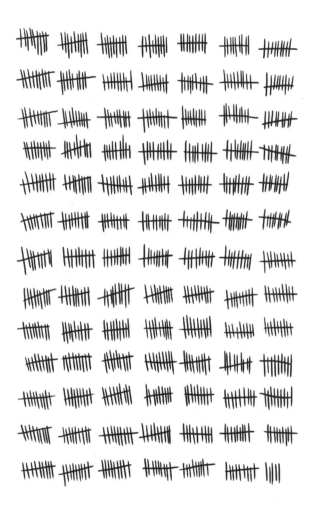

Dear Boris,

The man came back this morning, speaking in his language, smiling as only he can, showing his bright white teeth. He offered to take me hunting one morning. He says he'll teach me how to shoot and that it's so thrilling to see how the boars run when you aim at them and how their boarlets follow, whimpering. And you should've seen his eyes light up when he explained how when the little ones start chasing their mother, that's when you shoot the boarlets, one by one, in the belly. His mouth was watering, Boris; he smiled, imagining the baby boars with their guts hanging out, giving them to my mother as an offering, a gift for the new home: the best welcome to a new world that began in my dad's bed, beside my mother, in my house. And he would change the filthy old bedspread for a boarskin blanket, polished, waxed and very soft. His arrival would straighten life out, give meaning to Mother's body, Mother's garden, Mother's language.

I told him no fucking way. And my mum looked at me, frightened, and her eyes asked me to stop and I stopped. Meanwhile, she took some coins off the table and put them slowly into the pocket of my robe, without making any noise, as she challenged me with her gaze. The man was suddenly silent; he didn't know what to say or how to react. And I smiled with my whole body. You're right: they don't know anything about anything, just sound and fury. He took it, Boris, he bit his tongue and took it!

36

But at the same time, Boris, his eyes scrutinise me, scrutinise us; his eyes transform us, and beneath his interrogating gaze we become what they want us to become. And it is difficult to flee from that, very difficult. Every gaze is his way of sparking a dialogue, of subduing us a little more, of asking us something that we don't know how to answer, because they are the only ones who have the answers. But it doesn't matter: today, what matters is that he took it, that he didn't see it coming.

I hope this makes you proud of me. There's shouting in the background, as I write to you; Vita and the old ladies two houses down are cheering. They are banging on pots and clinking glasses. As if they were celebrating with me, over what I'd managed to do. I can feel their shouts inside of me. As I write to you my heart opens as if it had a door, as if it were exploding and growing huge, enormous, so that you could enter it any which way. A wide-open door that waits for you, Boris, always. For us. For this language we speak, which is our home. I offer you my heart so you can enter it, and set up your furniture inside, and make it yours: its muscled walls are for you.

I miss you every minute.

GRAVE

Some men coming to the house and telling us we had to leave is the thing I remember of those first few days. When they knocked on the door my mother pointed to the trunk in the dining room, as my hiding place, and she ordered me to only breathe when I counted to ten, that every time I got to the number ten I could breathe if I did it through my nose and slowly. On my fingers, I kept track of the time I spent submerged, blind, and when I felt my lungs completely full, I released the air. I heard bits of conversation in a language I couldn't quite understand and my mother saying that she was alone, that she was a widow, that she had no children, and that she was staying. Through the keyhole I saw for the first time some men with shaved heads rummaging through the house, apathetically. A few minutes later they left. That night, Mother got drunk with Grandpa: they took down the photo that presided over the dining room and they burned it. The paper lit the embers. The light illuminated their smiles, which I saw as diabolical, the smiles of famished animals. The flames licked the metal walls of the stove and I smelled the scent of burning varnish. The day's final gleams reflected in their teeth. Then the embers died out, and Mum and Grandpa fell asleep with their heads resting on top of their arms on the table, cheeks and ears red, and all the bottles empty. I went to sleep without saying anything to them, but first I put the bottles out in front of the door, in the snow, so they wouldn't break them if they got up disorientated in the middle of the night.

STRENGTH

We stopped killing pigs after my dad died. In our house, he was the only one who knew how to slaughter. Vita had taught him how, when she was young and strong. But she still kept on slaughtering, and she celebrated with the old women who came for the festivities and with her sister with the weird face. She used to invite me, when I was younger, and I would watch her do it from a corner, in silence. Before I entered her house she would order me to clean all the mud off my shoes so the hill spirits wouldn't enter. I'd tell her: 'Mrs Vita, I don't go to the hill.' And she would say: 'Scrub 'em well, dammit!' She sank a knife into the pig's neck, it let out a sharp grunt, and blood started streaming, thousands of rats pouring from its aorta. They put a bucket beneath it for the blood to fall into. There were splatters and clots, and it streamed down Vita's hands and cheeks as if it were her own blood. She repeated: 'The silence of Our Lord takes shape as chaos!' Then, with the blood and dry bread, she cooked these big black balls that she stored the entire year, and added them to her broth, where they turned soft, and they were delicious because they tasted of salty pig flesh. I thought that by watching, I'd already learned how to slaughter. And later I said to Mother that we could kill one, and I repeated the steps in the garden with the oldest pig we had. But I stuck the knife in wrong and the pig started to grunt and wouldn't stop: it just shrieked and shrieked, and it looked like it was in torment as the blood poured generously from its throat. My mother grabbed the shovel and beat it to death, saying she couldn't stand the noise, and she didn't stop until its head was as smooth and shattered as a dry autumn leaf.

EDUCATION

From then on, everyone lowered their heads when passing our house, and crossed themselves, and looked up at the sky. Some even spat in front of the door – and then Mother would mop the entrance with bleach, with the severity she had when cleaning the floor and the furniture, and tears streaming down her cheeks. They looked through the windows indiscreetly, wondering how it had happened, who had found him, where he'd killed himself. I felt very sad, at first, but later I thought that if Dad had been alive, when everything began, they would have kicked us out, because they recruited the men for the dirty work under military orders, and their families had to leave the affected zone. His death saved us, in a way. But in that moment we didn't know all that would happen a few years later. We couldn't have known. As my mum sobbed her eyes out, I thought no, no, I can't possibly bear the burden of his suicide, not on top of everything else.

Another evening falls. And another. And it is now, when the sun toasts the ground, that I slice another vertical cut in the wood column, with my dad's jack knife. Not like last week, when I drew a horizontal line through nine marks as I imagined the last nine days disappearing from my memory. I erase them. With the long stroke that goes through them, I erase them. With each mark that accumulates beside the last, I erase them. One by one. Five more. Nine hundred and five days, since it happened. When more time passes, only prints and traces will remain: capsules of a distant life. Memories can be secured but the present cannot. I hear the door closing: the man with the shaved head leaves. I remember how I told him that no, I wouldn't go hunting with him. How he went silent. That expression. I look through the window at the row of houses: capsules of a proximate life. Vita always wears a handkerchief tied over her hair and waters the graves in her garden, each one with a huge splintery wooden cross that she paints in bright colours. There are three, and each one has a photo in a rusting silvery frame. The smallest grave is her son's, who died at two years old. She often says: 'Saints preserve us, he would be alive now, and I could feed him.' She also says: 'Silly boy, I love my homeland and my graves. If I hadn't returned quickly, I'd already be dead.' And when she speaks, loudly, since she's missing her bottom teeth, she always sprays saliva. She works the garden with her hands, which are larger than her head, and when she covers her face with her palms it's very funny because she's like a giant hiding behind a rock, her fingers are so rough and thick.

PATH

My mother still hadn't come back from shopping – she'd gone to the butcher's with a short wooden cane that they scored for each piece she took, to keep track of the pieces they owed her in exchange for the pork she'd brought them months earlier. I will find my dad hanged like a calf in the middle of the dining room. The evening air breathed like an old lung among the handful of houses squeezed up against the back of the little hill. I will arrive with the sole desire to disappear and I will open the door with the lethargy of an old dog. Grandpa had gathered blackberries from the brambles near the house and was drinking spirits at the barracks. I will walk through the hallway and when I reach the kitchen, from a distance, I will see a frightened face with open eyes: my dad's. That afternoon had been like any other afternoon and, along the path, animals sank into the snow as they ran away from humans. I will only sense his body, a tired punching bag; his naked feet; his sleeping hands. Boris and I had talked for a long time on the way home and, when we parted, a pain had risen in my chest. I will freeze, just gleaming eyes and orange light burning the snow. I had thought, before opening the door, how I liked him so much and all of me twinged when I thought of him, but at the same time I was repulsed when he got together with the other boys and could be exactly like them. I will remember nothing more than my father's face, which will haunt me from then on, his bright black eyes like wild fish eggs. I was mumbling, on my way to the kitchen, filled with images of what I wanted to experience with Boris. I will close and open my eyes, trying to see the scene more clearly; but failing. I closed my eyes and opened them, keen, exploring my desire with an inner gaze: there was Dad.

'We'll drink and drink and drink some more
and whosoever laughs at us, we'll pummel!'

From the bedroom, you can hear the shouts of the old women who gather at Vita's home for supper today, which is a special day because they've just slaughtered a pig that they'll divide up and make last a whole year. The roasted ground is now black under the shadows of the full moon. I hear her sister with the weird face, wailing: 'Farewell, brain, until tomorrow!' and the liquor slides down their throats, not seeming to burn them, just carrying off their souls, a little stronger and rougher, like Vita's scabby hands. She goes out into the garden and takes the photos off the wooden crosses. She brings them into the dining room. Together they sing:

'Let's dance! I'll save my crying for my wedding day!
You all will have been forgotten.
Play that accordion! Play, my little dove!
Don't abandon your girlfriend,
the way my lover left me in bed!'

And I plead: 'Don't let him leave me alone, don't let him leave me, can you imagine? What would you do?' And one of the old women hits the hoe against the ground, and another grabs the rake and bangs it against the pot where they boiled the potatoes, and the air is filled with clamour. They sing together. And one of them says: 'Damn, you forgot the one about the mother who gave birth to her daughter in the middle of the field!' And a moment of silence is drawn up, as if they'd suddenly all died, but then they burst into song again together, compelled by a new force, even louder:

'Walk, walk, through the field,
a tyke or a tuber, who can tell!'

It starts to rain, the kind that erases the trees, the roofs, the silhouettes in the windows, even the shadows of the full moon. The women keep shouting while I fall asleep.

BLOOD

I went back and forth between fear and the clarity of a
fate that progresses clearly, and I reflected, night and day,
on how I could rid myself of that complicated inheritance.
When I went with my mother to the city or when people
came to the house to bring us something, they would say to
me: 'You look so much like him,' and there, in line for hot
food, my hands and lips icy cold, trying not to get angry,
not to spit on the old woman who pinched my cheek and
repeated: 'You look like him, you look too much like him.'
I held it in: 'Shut your trap, old lady, forget about me, leave
me alone. Eat shit, old lady, close that wrinkled old mouth
of yours for once in your life.' I stared at her just so she
would see the fire raging in my eyes, and know that it was
for her. When I got home, I helped my mother chop the
vegetables and store them, gut the rabbit, and mince it,
burn the hairs off the cuts of pork, and discard them. Later,
when I was stretched out in bed for the rest of the day, I
rubbed my arms with bleach, I rubbed hard and prayed,
promising myself that I wouldn't be like him – one of the
ways that I resisted that life sentence. At the same time,
I understood him: because here everything stretches out
long, and flat; it extends like a never-ending carpet. And life
is often like that, too long. As I scratched at my raw flesh
with my fingernails, I understood that the worst thing that
can happen to a son is turning out just like his dad. As if
the father were writing: 'Remember: blood doesn't expire.'
But my mother kept scrutinising my eyes and my mouth,

staring at me, comparing her worn hands – a sign of a time that is ending – with mine, and she struggled to find a trace of herself in my distanced body, which was like a warped mirror before her own; she grew silent, and turned her gaze to the spots and wrinkles on her old fingers.

In the morning, with the fog covering everything, Vita gathers up the bottles from the day before: another row in front of the door. Now bottles of air. As if the old women didn't drink. When really if I'd swallowed a fraction of what they'd guzzled, my throat would be bloody and raw. They must have left in the small hours. There is nothing to fear here, even in the darkness: just watch out for the wolves, the murmur of their splashing in the puddles left by the rain. 'Grandma is going out fishing. Let's sit down, my friends, and rest before undertaking the long road. Fishing poles: let's grab the simplest ones. Today there won't be many fish, there will be nothing after the rain. The river will be nervous. But be bold, Vita, be bold! Let's go fishing. That's it, good woman!' She speaks out loud because she has no one to speak to and I can hear her, from my bedroom. She passes by the front of the house and heads towards the river, which skirts the hill and leaves tranquil pools where the fish stop to graze. She returns with her basket full. Today, as always, when she looks up at my window, I hide behind the curtain because I know that if she doesn't see me, she will leave me some by the door, and later I'll fetch them and I can cook them, and I will eat them all by myself.

SHOT

With all the gobs of spit and my mother mopping frantically, I thought about Vita's sister, the one with the weird face, and Vita, always by her side. Because before the city emptied out and before the sickly air, they used to spit at her too, and then Vita told her not to leave the house anymore. To stay locked in there forever. But when the people fled and we were the only ones who stayed, and the grass grew and the animals returned from the forest, she started coming out again. After finding the fish dead, and the birds dead, and the plants dead, my mother said that she, so fragile and so strange, shouldn't do it. And then finally I saw her face, which I had never been able to contemplate in its entirety, because before Vita locked her up she always wore a scarf that hid it. There were no gobs of spit on our door any longer. No one walked past our window examining some beam. Mother no longer had to mop. Or hide. Perhaps that was why the man with the shaved head always came. I don't know. But when those things stopped happening, there was no mystery as to why, it was simple: everyone was gone. And that's what happens, when people leave: they take their rabid rage with them. Just like Grandpa used to say: the strongest, most powerful god is other people when they look at you.

RITUAL

Not his body: I more remembered my way of approaching him, of avoiding him, of fleeing him and fearing him because I didn't know in what shape I would find him. A constant metamorphosis towards something more diffuse, more distant, more ethereal. One day, at the back of the garden, in front of the gate, very still, talking to himself: all of him a black scar on all that green. A wound exposed to the wind and weather. One night, stretched out on the upholstered piece of furniture we use as a sofa, naked, not knowing what he was doing there, nor what he had done to end up like that. One early afternoon, shaved completely bald, when I saw his skull for the first time and didn't understand what paths could have led him to tear out his hair and reveal his sick eyes even further: could his demolished brain sense when it was noontime, or when it was night, or when it was dawn? One evening, when he climbed the hill, I got up to follow him – the crickets grew silent behind us – and when he reached the river, he watched it for hours, waiting as if the air were eroding him. I didn't understand it, and he explained it to me by saying that when sadness grows weary and disappears, then sadness is time. And my dad carried time within him. And once he was dead I didn't miss having a dad I could call 'Dad' because I'd never been able to call him 'Dad'. And all I was left with was a mystery rooted in everything I hadn't had time to understand because I was too young, and I wouldn't be able to understand those things, even after time, because the memory was already a vague shape that had been weakly etched in me: any thoughts, later on, would be thoughts based on that poor copy.

'My mum planted marigolds
and taught me to sing songs of springtime
about hope blooming.
Come, come, fishes big and small!'

REMAINERS

My dad drove to one of the rapeseed fields: a yellow sea. When the wind moved the stems, it seemed like they were crying. They grew beyond the houses, in the opposite direction from the city and the hill. There were swarms of bees that moved like the clouds. We made oil from those plants that wasn't meant to be eaten, but we ate it. We sowed poison and wheat grew. And we were all nourished by that bread. He told me that he'd brought me there to talk about men's things. When we got out of the car, he picked a flower, crushed it in his hands; a liquid dripped from between his pressed fingers and he said: 'That's what a man does.' Some friends of his came. I don't know if they were friends or men he drank with. What they asked me to do there isn't important, not now. We returned home with my dad repeating that he had cured me, and I celebrated it too: Dad said that he had cured me and I couldn't help but be happy. It fulfilled him. I fulfilled him. A sensible child that pleases his parents. But when you don't pay attention to things, they grow faster. And when, over time, Dad saw that I wasn't on the right path, that that ritual was long past and I was forgetting it, he reminded me: 'Lock that door, you have to always be doubly vigilant against vice.' And it's as if the more I bent my body against his will the more it bounced back, like a young reed. And that was what happened with my dad and me: the nice memories I kept of him always had a long shadow darkening them. And the moments that, when my memory didn't betray me, I found lovely, the more I thought about them, the less lovely they were.

For Mother. I do it for my mother. But she won't eat it, and I'll have to save the fish for dinner, when it'll be dried out on top and soggy with sauce and a fly might have landed in it. But I can't not go fishing even though I've already eaten the fish Vita left for me. When I reach the river pool right beyond the garden, I find her. Again. As if slicing the day, from just one she makes three or four different ones. I don't say anything about the fish – a secret that is ours and that we each keep privately. She asks me about the garden. I tell her I don't notice any difference. I ask her about the graves. Why it is that none of them look like her husband's. She replies that that man – her husband, but she calls him 'that man' – would have rotted the soil, buried there, and that the fruits on the trees would have grown poisonous. That he was a drunk who took her money. 'I only know how to speak: I cannot write or read. That was how he punished me. Then one day I slipped away and went to find Grandma at her house. I was there quick as a wink. I asked for her permission to leave him. And she told me that no woman in our family had ever left her husband. She explained that if a calf is born a certain way, hobbled, it'll always be like that, hobbled till the very end. Who could bring someone into this world like that, so damn broken!' She laughs the way witches do and I see her dark mouth, a tunnel. Then she sings a song about fish and springtime that I can no longer recall.

TREES

I found the man in the forest, like I found my dad that day: a scar on all that green. I was coming from the garden pond, where I had been contemplating the movement of the water and the shadow of the weeping willow on its surface, like a lance slashing through the tedious, circular current of the solitary and lush life we were living. Ascending the path I saw him, from a distance, so vegetal that he blended in with the pine trees and the bark, his dark skin so crusty and dry. He was dragging his frustration along with his baggage and weariness, his life accruing on top of his shoulders. When he saw me, he called out to me in my language, but with an accent I'd never heard before – distant, as if spoken in a place where it never rained. He was the first person who asked me about the back door to the Factory, when I barely knew of its existence. I didn't know how to respond; I scarcely understood what he was asking me, because a hesitation had taken hold of my body: what was the meaning of that man's passage through the world? Then the darkness began to shift in gentle, gleaming shapes.

I whispered to myself, repeatedly,
'Day nine hundred and eight':

My dear Boris,

You are right, you are right. It's true that this is my opportunity to do what you asked of me. For you and for me. And, that way, there will be no suspicion. No shadow. I adore the way you explain it: I believe it is possible. I took your advice and today, when he came back, I told him sure, we can go hunting whenever, that I know a tranquil area in the forest that we can reach by following the less torrid part of the river, and that that's where the boars always drink and rest with their babies. If nothing changes, we will go there next week, when he comes back to visit my mum. We'll go there nice and early. The sun won't have come up yet, so we can walk unnoticed: then, Boris, that's when I will do it. My mind is made up. And I will do it as you asked me to, following the steps you've described. For you.

Sometimes I think that you are a threat to me, I must admit. But other times I think you aren't at all, and that I like having heard, at some point, that you were a threat. Because of what you tell me and because of how you tell me it. And because of what must come, the results that remain a mystery to us. I don't even know why I'm writing this to you. But right now I'm nervous and have strange thoughts because I don't know exactly how I will do it, do all you ask of me. There are moments when I'm very happy and others when I'm very nervous and others when I think no, no way, and I think that I shouldn't do it because it's madness.

But you're right, the heart doesn't lie because it only speaks to us in one language, and we don't have our miseries, nameless and wordless, within our chests. This heart of mine always opens to the same place, the same place as ever, and there inside, people like him cannot enter. They can't. And I will not allow it. And this house of mine is my heart, my tongue, and this house of mine is not his.

Yours.

My mother is no longer in this world: it's as if she lives in some purgatory where the days pile up on a long, wide shelf, stored in drawers one above the other, separated without contact, without memory. They crumble there; her days will not lead her to any heroic place nor to any memorable deed. As if she repeated to herself that there's no point in searching for anything, because everything is exactly the same as everything else: languorous, pale, parched. Faced with a slow and shrivelled cosmos, always with the same expression, with a strength that can emerge only from indifference, because she is absolutely devoid of hope. She already knows that with hope comes failure, so without hope she assumes a possible victory. I'm explaining it this way in order to understand what I didn't understand before. First, that her despondency is in harmony with her anaemic body. Again: incredibly strong, because it is absolutely devoid of hope. Second, that you have to be that way in order to tolerate half a life spent working in the Factory. What I don't remember is whether the Factory made her that way or if she was already like that before she ever set foot in there.

Vita, always wearing that scarf. Every time I saw her I couldn't help but think of the women who were like a line of Vitas with scarves, crying, letting out the tears they carried within them, in front of the military SUVs, which were also in a row, and the women cried because their daughters were being carried off, and some women were being forced to leave, like Vita and her sister. They told them: It's not safe to stay here. And hit the road, make tracks. Some women cried, covering their eyes with shame and grief, and others traced sad farewell gestures. And, meanwhile, some men unspooled the roll from hell, as Mum called it, so that no one could come back, the concertina razor wire, which rusted a few months later, to the point of corrosion. And I've heard Vita repeat on several occasions that everyone should be able to live where their soul wants to. That people only die of anguish, and not of anything else. And that if you want to return home, no matter how much wire they put in your path, you will return there. And she did. And I've also often heard her praying: 'Where am I from? My house is my homeland. And in my homeland I will never get sick.'

All that's left of the Factory is the building, skeletal and in ruins. Sick. If the wind blows towards the mountains and I look through the window, I can glimpse it. Just the tip, because the Factory enters the ground and sinks beneath the world. From outside, before, you could only see the white, square entrance, with a door where the women entered in a line. On it was written, in large black letters, the word PURITY. The atmosphere smoked and the Tet river, which passed behind it, turned grey, and fish floated in it, and the ones who didn't had three eyes, or four, or two tails. My mother had explained to me that, at the Factory, time was different, that the earth swallowed it up. I would walk her there, we would say goodbye a fair distance from the entrance, and I would see the women entering in a line, languid and with white skin, as if they showered with bleach before work. Their skin melted inside there or grew cracked and dry. And if dreadful weather was approaching, pitch-dark sky and rain, they would have had no idea, because there was a different climate inside there. A different world. The stories of the subsoil, I knew them not. In fact, my mother refused to explain it to me until the town was left deserted; and it always seemed like she was only telling me a watered-down third of the story. Then, when all that was left was the handful we are now, and the Factory was starting to collapse, she said she would tell me. But all she explained was that thanks to the Factory there was light on the streets, and in the houses, and that that was how we could have a refrigerator, and a washing machine, and live almost like they lived in the city. About those people who went in through the back door, she didn't say a word.

PLAGUE

Vita, angry, singing over and over again:

'If a tank goes passing by
to show off its hard shell
we need to show it why
we'll send it straight to hell!'

My mother washes the dinner dishes, leaning over, moving her body with momentum, gripped, biting down on her lips from the effort, red from the blood that throbs through her flesh, scraping the bottom of an old pan with the aluminium scourer. Later, she sighs wearily, and extends her back, stretching up like a rush, and continues with the evening. Half contented, because I told the man with the shaved head that yes, I would go hunting with him. Arriving home from the Factory, she would straighten up and start again: another life. She'd leave some trace behind, at the door to the house. Start again: another life. When she explained some oddities about the Factory, I felt a world opening up, a world I was already aware of, because, inexplicably, I could sense what happened down there, below, in the bowels of the city and of the hill. Like when I was little and, after my mother had been swallowed up by the entrance, I crept over to the mouth of the bright white building against her orders and saw a shiny track of blood coming out, like a trail of sugary syrup. I ran home and instead of feeling the satisfaction of a puzzle piece fitting into place, it was more like a gust carrying off dry leaves, the dusty earth, the smaller insects and me along with it all, scared like a puppy hearing its mother's howl for the first time.

PRESENT

When Vita came back, we explained to her that it was the same, still, but with fewer people. The men mix alcohol with water, still, so it doesn't burn as much as it slips down their throats. They pass around the women and they touch the same flesh, still, in that house that serves as a tavern and where each morning, at the door, the empty bottles are piled up. We hear the bells from the Factory, still, the ones that used to signal the women's changing shifts. They've never stopped chiming. I hear them from my house, still. There is no longer any waiting in line for a bit of warm food in the freezing cold. Nor is there any trace of that house.

TEST

Piecing together what my mother told me, the boom-boom of the people, what Grandpa bellowed, the hidden truth that dominated the city, and the murmur of the forest and the animals, I began to understand the Factory. Understand that when night suddenly becomes day it is because of a mistake: normally those surges of energy were done during daylight, so people wouldn't see them. Sometimes, they happened at night. But not often: not enough for us to know for sure what was going on, but enough for us to have formulated our own theory, unfounded and premature, that drifted among the people. I also understood that if the city was clean, as those in charge claimed, it was because there was another entrance to the Factory, one that was right in the middle of the forest, on an out-of-the-way crest, a dead corner hidden both from the city's skyscrapers and from the few houses squeezed up against the side of the little hill. Through that door entered the fuel, so to speak, which wasn't liquid, or black, or sticky: it was files of people who flowed into that place without knowing where they were being led. I only knew that because on our way home Boris had shown me a photo of those people filing in. It was a citrus dusk as we walked home from school, before we parted and I continued along the path that led to the houses, while he returned to his small apartment in the city. That moment of the afternoon in which the absurdity of our routine embraced us and, suddenly, being children became onerous. He told me that his father had taken the photo on one of his

68

frequent walks through the forest, dressed in dark colours, with other men, not returning home for many days. And then he would spend days developing and printing those photographs and studying them, locked in his room. And Boris had taken one out of his album and hidden it inside the pages of a book. He would say to me: 'Secret.' And in the photo, it's true, you could see a long row of people who didn't look like people.

GLARE

A flash of light. From between the solid concrete walls shrouded in white and protected by iron plating. A flash of light through an impenetrable wall, impenetrable unless by some unknown mythic force that had never been seen before. It was a night that became day, suddenly, with the glare that emerged from the mouth of the Factory. The sky lit up and the moon, stars, constellations and grey clouds disappeared. In a second, all was white. At the same time, the fuses blew, and the windows filled with faces looking up at the sky. Coming together at the same point: no point; a heap of light without origin or end; a tablecloth doused in bleach that had covered the firmament and extended in every direction. Like a funnel or an open window, the Factory incriminated itself. Those who drew near and stared at it burned their retinas and never saw again. But in the same inexplicable way, the light retreated back to its source, ingesting itself, and the darkness again swallowed the sky, except for the phosphorescent aura around the Factory. When my mother arrived home, in the early morning, she didn't say a thing: she changed her clothes, went to bed and slept. The next morning, silence. And the next after that. But a trace of an unearthly glow still upholstered the sky and covered it for ten days. Then, this present story, now.

I whispered to myself, repeatedly,
'Day nine hundred and ten':

Boris: I did it, I did it, I did it!

I'm trembling right now. There was mist and the sun hadn't yet risen. I was afraid to come across some wolf, or a bear, or a boar; I was nervous and afraid.

He arrived this morning when my mother was still sleeping. I was on the porch waiting for him, sitting. Right on time. I told him to follow me, and once we were in the back garden, we hopped over the rusty gate and took the road that heads up and to the left. Suddenly I felt I was with the enemy, there by his side. I thought he could shoot me at any moment and then just tell my mother, when she woke up, that I hadn't shown up and that he'd been waiting hours for me there on the porch, never seeing me. He asked me stupid questions and I responded coldly. Inside I was panicking that he would suspect something and strike first. It was hard, but I kept thinking about you and that calmed me down, because you'd told me many times that it would all go well if I didn't hesitate. And I didn't hesitate, Boris. I didn't hesitate even once. I remembered your instructions, I repeated them to myself, keeping them in the front of my mind. And I imagined how proud you would be to see your wish fulfilled. That I would be the one to fulfil your wish, Boris.

When we reached the spot, we got behind a large rock with a view of the tranquil part of the river. He said: 'It's hard to believe that the Tet, such an agitated river, can be like this.' A stupid comment. We loaded the rifles and we waited for the boars, who wouldn't come because I've never seen boars there. But he waited patiently for them. I told him that I was going to take a leak. After walking a few paces – bam! – I shot a hole in his shoulder at close range and he started to squeal like a pig. The echo of the shot took flight through the trees. I'm sorry I didn't have better aim. When I tried to take his weapon, he seized it by the barrel and hurled it at my face, knocking me to the ground. But a second later I had already grabbed his rifle and I rammed the butt into his cheek and he cursed his attempt to fight back. But then he gripped my ankle and held me fast; he had me pinned to the ground and was starting to crawl up my legs: then, point-blank, I shot him twice in the thighs and the blood started spurting out. You can just imagine how he screamed. He finally lost consciousness from all the blood and all the screaming. I tied him up the way you told me. I thought of you as I did it. May lightning strike me down if I didn't truss him up just as you said I should: he won't be able to move a finger when he wakes up. Then I went home.

I hid the rifles under some slabs on the bank of the slow part of the river, where I fish, and I swam to wash off the sweat, blood and nerves. The sun hadn't yet come up and my mother's blinds were still lowered. I changed my clothes and started reading in my bedroom. But I couldn't concentrate and I decided to write to you.

I'm trembling. I love you. All I can say is that I feel like I am climbing ivy that clambers up a building's face and, as it does, it fastens its roots along the cracks between the bricks. Growing is easy. What's difficult is halting the growth, stopping it. No matter where you cut that ivy, it's already planted its roots, and it seeks out the remaining dampness in the bits of moss and mould on the wall. How can it be stopped? But at the same time I pray for it to keep growing forever, because it fills the gaps and that's a good thing, that those gaps are filled – that I no longer moor myself only to you, but to the you that isn't there, and those clinging vines make the sameness not always the same, not always fall in the same place.

All that is to say, if only I were with you, and not with my mother, but I don't want to torture myself either, or collapse in self-pity. You know what, pay me no mind, forget what I said, erase it.

Yours always.

I can tell by the sounds of her going up and down the stairs: she's awake. When she sees me, she looks confused as to why I'm there. 'He didn't show up, Mother, have you heard from him?' And she points to my cheek to say that it is red. The coffee pot shakes in her hands; she scoops up coffee grounds with a trembling teaspoon, spilling more out than she gets in. She strikes matches and just as she's got them aflame, they snuff themselves out, one after the other. I light the burner for her. It strikes me that she looks like I did, just minutes earlier, writing to Boris with crooked handwriting and my pulse pounding a thousand times a minute, two thousand, three thousand, with my heart beating like a rabbit's, in my corneas, in my ears, in my sex. She tells me she hasn't heard from him. And she rests her lips on the edge of the mug. Over the next few days she will go out on the porch, bright and early, and wait all morning for him. She will get dressed, comb her hair, and in her smoothed clothes she will sit on the chair for hours, with devotion, patience and hoping for the best. Waiting for him. And no, Mother, no. In two weeks from now, another man will deliver the letters and the pensions. She will smile when she sees him, wearing the same uniform. He will also have a shaved head. He will never speak our language. No, Mother, no: this one will have blue eyes and brows so blond they'll be almost impossible to see.

CALVARY

The first building they sealed off was the Factory: the women, quickly, went home, packed up their clothes, shut the suitcases and followed their husbands wherever they led. And it was the first place where the abundant grass began to grow, and the first place that started to crumble, because no one took care of it, and we watched it glow from a distance. But only the facade collapsed, falling into pieces and deteriorating at the same pace as my mother's features. You could see its skeleton of rusty iron and reinforced concrete. But we've never been able to enter its insides: the doors, impenetrable; the walls, barriers metres thick. Now there are people who journey there in an eternal pilgrimage from places you would never expect: they come and leave flowers at the entrance. Some spend the night there, sleeping rough. Others, when they arrive, caress the walls and return home, hundreds of kilometres away. Which is why I sometimes find strangers in the forest: they are looking for the back door. I've never found it.

Nervous, my mother drinks her coffee in one swallow. It's as if she'd just lost Dad's ring among the garden grass, or amid the furrows, and searching for it entailed the danger of finding Grandpa or some other remnants of an ancient memory. Nothing calms her. She opens the door to go out into the garden, the empty mug in her hands. The screen door slams. From the kitchen, through the door frame, I see Vita's sister chasing our cow through the meadow beside our garden, with her tongue out and her eyes gleaming – the tongue and eyes of the sister, not the cow. The cow walks impassively and flicks her tail between her legs, whipping them to scare off the flies. She grazes, imperturbable, lowing and ignoring the moans of the sister, who clings to her and strokes her, and touches her ears, and searches out her udders, and rubs her sex. She takes her by the head and looks into her eyes: the meeting of two warm breaths. My mother continues looking into the empty mug, while the sister speaks to the cow in a strange language only she understands. The cow keeps grazing, indifferent, and the sister continues, accustomed as she was to indifference. My mother closes the door with a bang and I hear her as she walks to the end of the garden: 'Get away from here, you filthy beast!'

EARTHWORMS

When anyone asked Vita if she was afraid, she would answer: 'I'm not afraid of anything, kids.' Then she amended her answer, saying: 'Except for hunger.' When they asked her if she felt lonely, she would respond: 'I haven't got even one man my age left here. I'm right as rain.' Then she amended her answer, saying: 'Yeah, sure, there are a couple, but they're worthless.' When they reproached her for sometimes using her shovel to bash the men who brought her pension, she would respond: 'I was scared shitless.' And they reminded her that she'd said she wasn't afraid of anything. 'I was scared shitless that they'd come back here again, that they'd take me to another house where the sun rises from a different place.' And she added: 'They destroyed all of me, except my soul. You don't know this, so I'll tell you: when I came back, I grabbed a fistful of dirt, as Our Lord is my witness, and I promised I'd never budge from here again. Amen. A good fistful of damp earth! This land of mine is a sight to behold. And even if it weren't, it's mine.' And it doesn't matter if your hands get dirty, because if you get them dirty, you can always wash them later.

I suppose that what binds my mother and me isn't blood or place, but our shared history, and our distrust of the future. And also what ignites inside me when I look at her: that I want to remember her, despite everything. It happened today: after the years of mourning, we face each other, holding our coffee mugs, our hands trembling, our bodies trembling; my body still pulsating with the charge of what I've just done. I remember the bond that links us and despite the destruction, I still yearn for that love. Similarly, I realise I've lost the true memory of my dad. I remember my version of the things he did and the things he said, of what he meant to me. But I don't remember the tangible meaning of who he was, his presence, how he modulated his voice, what colour his eyes were. And I've thought, now too, that the same thing will end up happening to me with my mum. Sooner or later, the same thing will happen.

I whispered to myself, repeatedly,
'Day nine hundred and fourteen':

Dear Boris,

Today I saw a wolf's eyes up close. I was heading towards the river to find water for lunch: my mother wanted to make broth with hen bones. And there it was, drinking thirstily from the drums that we'd left to collect rainwater. Maybe it was a she-wolf, I don't know. We stared at each other for a while. It didn't seem like an animal. And I understood that I didn't seem like a human to it: it perceived me as a large hairless beast. With my eyes I asked: 'What do you want, what do you want?' and it responded. Really, I swear. But I couldn't understand the response, of course. We looked at each other for so long that I couldn't even tell you how long it was. I believe you, now, believe what you told me the other day, that you'd seen wolves parading on the hill and hiding among the brambles. Do you think they know we're here? Do they know that we won't hurt them, no matter what? As I was looking at the wolf, I thought, I'm incapable of living, I don't know enough. Maybe because of this thought, my gaze shifted and the wolf headed up into the forest. It leapt over the pen and disappeared into the brambles and the ferns. Not a trace.

I brought in the pot filled with water and I told my mother that, while the broth bubbled, I was going to check on the traps I'd set up in the forest, make sure they were still intact after the river flooded its banks. And I went to search for the man with the shaved head. I retraced the wet path to the left, until I found him. The forest smelled of teeming life. Rays of light slipped through the leaves and illuminated swarms of mosquitoes. My feet slid on rotting leaves. I looked up towards the sky, a ceiling of green boughs, and the gaps where the light slipped in were like faults in the earth, flat and infinite. The world was as tranquil as a fish tank. Nothing had happened: not before, not after that moment. The breeze moved the tender stems calmly. And there he was.

His lips were pale lilac, his clothes soaked, and he was barely moving. He didn't say anything to me: he just looked at me. I gave him a piece of bread. I don't know why. I'd brought it for myself but I offered it to him. He chewed it, and when it was a pasty liquid mass, he spat it into my face. He said he would kill me and then I felt scared, because his face was furious as he said it. It seemed as if it could be true, that he would wriggle out of the ropes and kill me by bashing my head in until juice came out of my head. I'm sure he was thirsty, but I didn't ask. I looked at his hands: the ropes were intact. And I walked back the same way I'd come. Then he started screaming but I kept going and his screams became softer. Eventually, I could no longer hear them.

The sun had come out and a vapour slipped through the wet leaves and ascended through the branches. The forest was full, heavy. I stood for a little while looking at the leaves. Deep down, I've always needed to understand the reasons behind everything, even when others have already beaten me to it, even when I've resigned myself to the silences. But today, Boris, today there is a natural order that extends in every direction: in his tired eyes; in his weak voice; in the leaves, a watery mat on top of the forest; in the river, filled with fish after the rain. And I wanted to listen to the world, understand it. Sometimes you have to take destiny into your own hands, and that's what I did, Boris. Later an unfathomable winter will come and, *then, again, another spring, and we can't imagine how it will be or what misfortunes it will obscure amid the growing plants, but I will have taken destiny into my own hands. And I will be able to say it. I will be able to say it to you.*

You are a force.

INVASION

I remembered another photo that he'd showed me, of when we still went to smoke and drink on the porch at the house of one of those other guys. I only joined in when Boris invited me, very few times. A tree's branches had come through the railing and its dry leaves had fallen onto the chairs. Boris would grab his camera and make nature expand; it wasn't alive, he was the one who moved the stones and reproduced the hills and multiplied the boars, with his camera – where does he begin and his camera end? And I was about to write to him that it was lovely and brought back a lot of memories, but I didn't – I couldn't remember anything about that moment, I was just obsessed with it and wanted to return there by any way possible. But when you think of an experience as lovely, here, it must mean that you are experiencing it wrong. Nothing can be lovely here. Not now.

Cooking is a distraction for us. Mother doesn't stop moving all day long so she won't notice the time. How it rises. How it falls. Especially now, now that her nerves are shot. She asks me: 'Do you think he'll come back? Do you think?' She cleans, cooks, sweeps the stairs, polishes the porch. Straightens the roofing sheets. She pulls up the weeds that grow along the edges. Today for lunch she made onion soup. We also threw in some croutons made of dried bread and the broth from the hen bones, boiled for the third time. But she was an old hen, so she still gave taste to the soup. When I was little, when my dad was here, we would put everything into the pot, everything we had. The steam clouded the window and I rubbed my hands over it, to see the hill. I go to get water from the river in the summers. In the autumn, we get our water from the rains; and in winter we melt snow because the river, slender as a thread, freezes from the surface to the bottom. The broth comes out just as transparent. As if it hadn't been simmering for three hours. My mother smiles. She doesn't smile often, but when she does, she still can't hide her grief, as if she knew that all joy, at some point, ends as sadness. We save the remainder at the bottom of the pot, in the cool shadows. When the Factory closed, we were left without light. The first summer was easy. It was during the winter that we suffered. And that was when the looting in the city began too, the long silences, the suspicions, the laws each person took into their own hands. Then, my mother would talk about the Factory more than ever: of when they built it with the scaffolding, the bricks, those ladders and the razor wire going through the trees, viciously attacking the landscape and wounding it. And the result: the white skeleton that emerged from inside the earth, amid the blue.

HANDS

There was another story about Vita, everyone told it everywhere, and it was about when they came looking for her one day to take her to Mass in the military cart that gathered up the old ladies on the first Sunday of the year. About how she brought liquor in a felt bag, wrapped with rags so the bottles wouldn't clink. The cart showed up, filled with the Vitas and their scarves. It moved slowly along the paths and the roads. Vita clung to her bag with both hands, protecting it like a newborn baby. With every jolt she closed her eyes and prayed for the bottles not to make a noise. The cart dropped the women off at the church, and when she found herself before the man who blessed the things that were brought to him, a man curiously muscular beneath his white tunic, she told him: 'I want to bless my moonshine. Where can I do that?' The man replied: 'No.' And Vita tried again: 'Well, dammit, wine can be blessed. Why not my moonshine?' And the man replied: 'It's not allowed, hide it.' And she insisted: 'Everything is allowed. Anything can be blessed.' Vita didn't believe what they told her in that dark church; she prayed to another god who was everywhere and had no form.

After washing up and throwing out the hen bones – finally – beyond the river, I watch my mother from the bedroom window. She says that after eating she needs to move, or the sluggishness of the afternoon will overtake her and she'll slacken like an animal. Her eyes are murky, a veil covering them, and she rips weeds from the garden, tired. Whenever I look through the window, she is ripping out weeds with hooded eyes. She bends over with one hand on her lower back. With the other she grabs the plant by its stalk, extricating it with a residual power she summons from deep in the muscles of her bad back. She walks over to the pepper tree and sits beneath it for a while – the plastic chair cracking open – and crosses her arms below her breasts, holding them up. The afternoon darkens as I watch her there, from my window, and the sunlight traces shadows on one side of her face, drawing her nose long and pointy, and then the other, giving her a rounder and more tranquil profile. I wonder about the extent of her pain and whether she could carry the weight of it all. She is not a tall tree with deep roots – like the sturdy pepper tree she sits under, which was already around when I was born – but merely has the tiny, petite body of a fragile pigeon. I think: What is she waiting for? What is she doing with her hands? Perhaps she is cupping them together to create an empty space, so that a god can enter. Then I close the window and stretch out on the bed. Like every day at dusk. And I write to Boris.

NECKLACE

When I was little, the man who blessed the things brought to the city came to our district to perform. And those in the blue house, at the end of the street, watched him from their terrace, half hidden. He delivered this performance at the start of every season. He would begin by shouting: 'Better it is to be of humble spirit with the lowly, than to divide the spoils with the proud.' I already understood then that he was saying that because we were the lowly, and he had to tell us in order to console us. And later, when he had finished, I would go over to him and stroke the gold pendant that hung around his neck. When I touched it for the first time, I asked him what was inside it, because it was very heavy. He approached each of the children who lived there – there weren't many of us – and he touched our heads with both palms together, and muttered: 'I bless thee.' And he ordered the parents to have more children, because otherwise those houses would become a filthy rat-trap of old folks. And he wasn't wrong, no: after what happened, in the city, the houses, the forest . . . most of those left there were old and tired people.

FERTILITY

It wasn't particularly difficult to understand what he meant, the religious man who blessed us and heard our confessions. He had a phrase he told us, about what he feared we might do. If he thought that from this corner of the world we could rise up, he would tell us: 'A wicked man taketh a gift out of the bosom to pervert the ways of judgement.' And if he wondered whether one of us could light a spark, he would recite to us: 'Let a bear robbed of her whelps meet a man, rather than a fool in his folly.' And if he feared some spontaneous loss of control, he resorted to urgency: 'A man shall not be established by wickedness: but the root of the righteous shall not be moved.' Everyone believed him, and waited for his arrival, when the snow melted, or when the rain ceased to adorn the roofs with pearly drops, or when the sun ruled again. And I struggled to understand it, how everyone believed in him so firmly, because he kept returning and repeating that refrain: 'The surname of this land is Opportunity,' but no one had ever set foot there. Before leaving, he would remind us: 'Do not forget that there is but one true image. There are no others. Taking photographs is dangerous.' And I, of course, imagined that he was referring to the one we had hanging in the dining room. Because, at that time, I had never seen another.

In my bedroom, I reread Boris's letters. I would prefer to do what my mother does to kill time – cook, clean, sweep, buff, polish. Move my body to avoid facing it. Kill time. Kill rage. I reread Boris's letters and sense that he doesn't experience things the way I experience them. Perhaps because he has no one else to love beyond himself, perhaps because he has preoccupations that have nothing to do with me, or with him, but with the world. He's never felt part of this 'us' where they pointed at me, in which unhappiness seems to cling like the smell of garlic on your fingers. I don't know who we are, this 'us', but I've kept scraping away at it and I do feel included: the bent. The deviants. The dissolute. The pole smokers. The doomed. Later, I understood that this unhappiness is not ours. That it is an outside gesture imposed upon us: that when I locked myself in the room with the tubs and the row of raw loaves, when I closed the doors so it would be dark and the day would be over, I wasn't imprisoning myself because I was sad, I did it because they wanted me to be sad. And that's different. They wanted me to hide everywhere, as if I didn't entirely live within myself. And I obeyed: and the heady scent of raw bran and the fertilising flesh went into my nostrils. And the silence: that love that dared not speak its name.

PUNISHMENT

When Boris would write to me about other things besides the photos, he'd say that all he needed was the rat room and a country to live in. And I often would respond that I understood what he was saying about the rat room: where else could we have met up, over such a long time, otherwise? But what I didn't understand is what he said about the country. And he said that I would surely understand it, someday. That if you're a rat, you don't want to live in a rat's nest, or in that fucking room, he repeated, you want to live in the countryside or in the shade of a henhouse, so you can shatter the eggs and eat them in their gelatinous state. Imagine you're a rat with your mouth dripping yolk-yellow and sated. Now imagine a rat's nest: a long passageway with no way out. Do you understand? And I didn't understand; Vita always trapped the rats that ate her eggs and hung them in front of the door so the other rats would see them and be deterred. And when she found a snake, she would cut it up into pieces and make them into garlands that she'd extend along the fence. And what if that happened to us? Boris, what if there were a Vita, in that imaginary country?

I whispered to myself, repeatedly,
'Day nine hundred and sixteen':

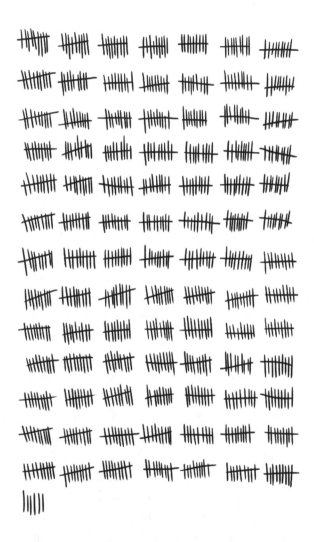

Boris,

If you asked, I would stop writing to you and stop giving such free rein to my feelings. I often think I reveal too much in these letters, expose myself more than I should, and that you aren't the one who should be reading them. I should just say that.

Today I went up to visit him again, before our meeting in the rat room. I took the same path as always, through the same forest, through the same trees as ever. I was the same as ever. But the lightning bolt is faster than the gaze. And the scent is faster than the thunder. A dark stench: of sour egg, of pigsty, of when Mother came home from working at the Factory and the odour entered the house to stay permanently, and no matter how many windows and doors you opened there was no way to get rid of it. Like a cloud, it moved towards me. And I was no longer following the path, I was following that smell, a clue. From a distance, I saw a fleshy mass, shapeless, tied to a tree. I couldn't recognise him. I approached. There were ripped clothes, scattered. As I got closer, I could make out some white dots, which were the bones. There were bite marks all over: the flesh, shredded. I drew even nearer, but the flies disgusted me and I didn't want them to touch me with their bloodstained feet and their beady heads dripping with rotting juices. His head was bowed and I leaned down to find his gaze: I failed because they'd emptied out his eye sockets. Did they start there, eating first the more tender, gelatinous parts of his body? Or could he watch as the little animals stripped off his flesh and he slowly bled out?

Beyond that: who had eaten him? The boars? The bear that wanders around hungrily after its winter hibernation? The wolves? Or a gang of violent raccoons with small teeth like the serrated edge of a bread knife? The wolves, the wolves. The wolf! Boris, do you think maybe it's the wolf I saw the other day, who devoured him whole? The one I stared at for a while in the garden, who came over to me, and who hadn't touched even one hen, or the cow, or anything? Was it the wolf, waiting for this man? A wolf who only eats this kind of flesh — hard and fibrous, difficult to chew; tough to tear off the bone. Every bite must be a thick, ripping tear, and I can already hear his screams, Boris, I can already hear them! And I'm gripped by something I can't describe, in my head, and it runs down my spine and reaches my toes and fills me with human sap, Boris, a sap that few people know, green and thick and primordial, more liquid than blood, faster and shinier, shinier, shinier than blood. The wolf!

It's done, it's over. Goodbye to this man with the shaved head, forever. Do you sense our fortune? We've changed the course of events and, why did we do it, Boris, if not to change the direction of our destiny, allied and bound together? Suddenly, our lonely separation, which already felt like a physical stab wound and had poisoned me, living by myself, and you, by yourself — suddenly it hurts less. And it is that sap I'm talking about. It is that light that now runs through our veins. It is that leap into the void, into the celestial that lives on earth, in the forest. What will come later? What awaits us, now?

I loved the time we spent in the rat room. I was missing you so much. I will treasure this envelope with your photos like a relic: thank you.

Sending you such love, Boris!

(I get goosebumps when I say your name: Bo-ris.)

Yours.

We meet in the room on the second floor, the one with the rats. Weeks have passed since the last time we saw each other. Until today, just letters. He shows up sweaty and dusty, walking from the city along the shortcuts through the forest. We call this place the rat room because the first time we came here, shortly after the house was abandoned, we saw rats with red eyes and bald backs that coiled their tails and shrieked. When we went into the room, they froze, petrified, playing dead. In that row of houses in the valley, against the world, there was only one that was large, and with wide picture windows, and terraces where they placed cages with colourful birds that would vanish when the winter came. The blue house. I saw the birds from my parents' bedroom window when it was warm, chattering with their sharp red beaks and beating their wings. Now, its gilded roof is rusty with age, the candelabra interwoven with spiderwebs, and beneath the dust hides glossy gold lacquer furniture.

UNIFORM

Since then, living has become surviving, which is the worst way of being alive. And loving, for me, has become learning how to stabilise an impossible desire. In our gardens we started to accumulate slats and wooden boards, scraps of corrugated roofing that now function as doors for the large cages, and we did with our dead what our strength allowed us to. Our currency was our word: hold out your hand and hope they don't punch a hole in it. The visits from outsiders were reduced to shipments and the pensions that the men with the shaved heads brought us. But sometimes other men came, dressed in dark grey rather than green, so we could easily tell them apart, and they gathered up our things to study. They said: 'This is science,' and we watched as they took a head of lettuce, a few eggs, a demijohn of water from the stream, bags they filled with air. They said: 'We have a special unit,' and we let them do what they set out to do, without asking ourselves if we believed them or not.

When we meet up, we smoke and don't talk much. Boris opens his moonshine and drinks, offers me some and I say no. Each time we see each other, the bottle is simpler and the alcohol worse: I can tell by the bitter taste of his mouth. He thinks in silence and I watch him. I want to ask him how he's been since the last time we saw each other, but I don't. We don't discuss what we write about in our letters, but I still feel upset that he hasn't said anything about the man with the shaved head, about what I did for him, about my efforts. And especially now, when I'd just come from making sure he was dead. Arguing is, often, the only way to get a word out of him – just a word, Boris, please, a single word – but today I don't have it in me. Silence: his way of fleeing. The rat room still has the curtains the owners put up there, burgundy velvet, now grey, covered in ash. We don't say anything to each other, we just are together and I hold him and then he kisses me, the way he does, hard, almost choking me with his kisses. He takes off his shirt and I take off my own, because we never remove each other's clothes, and I hold his arms, which are strong, unlike mine, but with some small red spots on the back, which I like to stroke; and I kiss his hair, of which there is little, and I like that. He grabs me by the hair really hard and when he grips me I think about how animals fuck, that they do it like this too, with this drive, without words, and when they look into each other's eyes, they open them so wide it's as if they're communicating with their gaze. Because if a rat were to see Boris and me, it would think we are two young beasts just learning about this, who don't want to speak a word when they meet up because they just want to touch each other, and pound each other, clumsily, and bellow, deep, like wild creatures.

CONTINUITY

That Mum worked at the Factory. That Dad always drank, with death at the bottom of every bottle. That the house where we lived was a bunch of boards, iron sheets and asbestos, of dust and wild animal hairs. That the hill separated my street from the city, where another, larger life existed. That a few metres further on there was the blue house, clean and big, but that its door was always, always, a few houses further on. That eating meant fishing, and slaughtering, and harvesting, and planting, and harvesting, and planting again. Again and again. That my body never managed to fulfil its duty to others' expectations, or mine, like a punishment. That I was another plate at the table – and three cannot eat as cheaply as two. Even my breathing was aggressive for the things they did to me in that specific way. But there are facts that can't be changed. And those facts, I couldn't change them: being poor made me equal to the rest of the poor, but living through those things made me different from those in the city, and those beyond the mountains, and the other boys who lived in all the countries around the world that I could imagine at that time.

We don't wipe the dust off each other either, when we've finished. Because our sweat dissolves the dust, and stings as it drips down the scratches on my back. It scares me, sometimes, that way he has of loving me. So wild, and I just let him do what he will with me, grab me by the arms, rock me back and forth, up and down, turn me away from him and then to face him. Both of us sweaty and in silence. We have to be careful with the broken glass on the floor and, quickly, we cover ourselves because the cold comes in through the windows, which no longer close. Then, we smoke again and we say a few words. He tells me that in the block of apartments where he lives there are only a few people left; and that even though so much time has passed, there is always someone who returns. We hear a door creaking and some footsteps coming up the stairs. Someone speaking. It is dark. We huddle in a corner, beside a red and gold chest. The door opens extremely slowly: the footsteps of someone entering. And I, with my eyes closed, murmuring to god in a whisper, now, so close and so far from home.

WAVES

When the sound grew crackly and the voices foggy, my mother exhaled a gasp of exhaustion. And I would tell her not to despair, that we had to keep trying. Both of us, at the table, without light, since the sun had already set and the cold came in beneath the door. I had found it while searching the first empty houses – that's what I'd told Mother. I had taken it from the blue house, the first time Boris and I had met up in secret there. He had taken the cans and the glass jars, and also some kitchen utensils. I had taken the radio home. It was quite small, it only took up half of the table, and my mother was surprised because she said that as a girl, when her parents took her to the tavern, the radio there was like a bureau, like a mattress up against the wall. We tried it out at night. Sometimes, we could hear voices clearly, but we didn't understand them, because they were in another language. And I was surprised because after listening to the radio my mother's face changed, as if she understood what they were saying. And when the next day came she would say to me: 'Let's try it again.' And we did. And I liked turning it on and searching for voices, because it was one of the few activities we did together, but I didn't understand why she wanted to try every night. When I went to sleep, I would dream that she did it to spend more time with me, that that made her happy. Later on, the radio stopped working and one night that winter, we burned it.

A weak, tattered man, whose ribs you could see beneath his scaly skin, as if they were about to burst through. He reasoned with himself, quite mad, talking to someone else; and vocalising his interlocutor's responses as well, in a higher tone: one minute he is angry, the next laughing, the next screaming with wide eyes. Then he sees us there in the corner, half dressed. At first, he is embarrassed. I laugh inside because he's the one who feels trapped, not us. But then he becomes infuriated, and his embarrassment turns to rage. He opens his eyes the way he'd opened them when angry with his non-existent interlocutor and he furrows his brow. I continue praying in a whisper and trust that Boris will take action. I entrust myself to him now, as if my life depends on him, pinching his arms to keep from screaming. But Boris is silent. Boris, Boris, Boris, say something – anything, but say something. And the man grows larger, shouting at us and calling us whores, and messed up, saying he'll burn us alive because we're contagious and sick, that our heads are rotted, and he'll kill us. I groan. Boris is silent. The man approaches. I stand up and slowly draw closer to him. I smash the bottle of liquor on his head, so hard you can hear his skull shattering. And I think about a thick branch of a tree splintering.

PROGRESS

Dad took me to the forest. He hadn't shaved in days and when I saw him like that he always seemed a bit mad because, behind his eyes, I sensed his weariness and his longing for drink. Before leaving he told me to grab my money, that he would show me a secret no one else knew about. I brought what I'd saved up from taking care of the garden for the owners of the blue house, a little bundle I carried in both hands, squeezing it tightly so I wouldn't drop it. The forest, then, was a dense greenness that frightened me, because it was a risk, and a deep well, and my loneliness in the midst of nature chilled me to my core, and it was so lush that I always feared it would swallow me up and absorb me, and that then there'd be nothing left of me. I released my grip with one hand so I could hold on to my dad. I clutched his T-shirt and pulled it taut. We reached some shade, far from home. He dug a shallow hole with his hands. His fingernails were always a little long and dirty. His hands served for digging, and for poking holes, and for working the way men do. He told me: 'I'm going to teach you how to make the money plant grow.'

That noise of crushing bone: a footstep atop the snow in our solitude, the crunching; and the blaze, later, crackling in the bonfire, the log that contracts from the flames and squeals. The rag-and-bone man had made not a peep. Not a trace of fear, seconds before, not a sign of pain, head held high, and he did not utter any last words. Just a free fall, onto the ground. There was no clatter, with his crumpling, that's how thin he was and how fragile his bones. Boris is frozen. He stands up and takes my arm. We leave the room slowly, because we both know that now we can never go back there, to the rat room. We go down the white marble stairs covered in shredded carpet and slippery with layers of dust. Before leaving through the kitchen window, Boris hands me an envelope, that I should open at home. We say goodbye with our eyes, not knowing when we'll see each other again. He steps on a glass pane and we both smile at the same time, because it sounds exactly like the shattering of that man's skull.

FRUITS

He told me: 'Give me your money.' And I gave it to him. He placed the little packet at the bottom of the hole and covered it up with dirt again. It smelled of grass, dampness and earthworms. He told me: 'You have to remember where we planted it.' I looked around, searching for a reference point to orientate myself, and I counted the trees, I took note of the rocks, the carpeted rotten leaves, the boughs, and I got nervous because I thought that I wouldn't know how to find that place again. He told me: 'In a couple of weeks, when you come back, the money plant will have started to grow.' I dreamt about it for days. It was like a thicker asparagus with coins hanging off it; and when the coins grew, the stalk would give, fold over and sink amid the other thin leaves. I went back. Fearfully, but knowing that double, triple the coins we'd planted were awaiting me, hundreds, and the coins gleaming, dripping from the bramble, like water. I found a hole. And there was just the rag at the bottom, untied and dirty.

As soon as I get home, I go up to Mother's bedroom, the only place in the house it is visible from. I see one of their parrots, magenta and lime green, with the imperial tail and big eyes. But no: a chiffchaff is making a nest in the rain channel and still a wild rose bush survives amid the ferns and brambles, and just sprouted buds – trees that burst with flowers when they know they are about to die. On the walls there is just dry ivy. With the envelope in my hands, I think about the owners, who fled as fast as their feet could carry them. The blue house, in those days, already had dark cornices and a derelict garden. They no longer had me take care of it. They hadn't had children. And the woman, in addition to her sad expression, seemed fatigued by having to put up with his parents, the indifferent visits of strangers and having to always smile in front of others. And later without the parrots, looking towards the garden as if she wanted to bring the plants back to life with her gaze. And, now, the house has descended into shavings, filled with rats and that man's head dripping blood. I open the envelope.

I open the envelope. There are several photos of Boris. When did he go to the seaside? How, and with whom? Why hadn't he told me about it? What were those rocks, and that water splashing them? I can place where some of them were shot. Others, he'd taken with me: one in the garden of the blue house, from the kitchen window where we enter; a small animal run over on a hard shoulder, not buried. And the sky, so many of the sky, of frayed clouds, stars and the sun collapsing against the earth. So many more. I hold them delicately, because there is a part of me that knows that, from the moment he looked into my eyes and said: 'Here,' he was offering me a poisoned gift, as if instead of photographs, in that envelope, there were razor blades. And his memory, about to explode in my hands: and what would I do with so much strange blood? Because he has his memory and I have mine and, together, we have nothing. Boris and I share only a declaration: the one that states that we will tell each other our lives in letters, that we will meet in the blue house and that we will love each other like animals. We decide what is important, and the rest, who cares. Not a single memory.

I whispered to myself, repeatedly,
'Day nine hundred and twenty-two':

Dear Boris,

How are you feeling? I'm well, but I'm constantly thinking about when I'll have time to write to you and be able to explain what I'm doing and how everything's going. And today, for example, it's Tuesday, but it seems like it's been a week since it was Sunday, but no. Mum says 'the day before yesterday' and I think sure, it's not possible that the day before yesterday was Sunday, but, actually, it was, and that's how time passes, like a map with no co-ordinates. And the brain's bewilderment and misunderstandings only grow, and suddenly I've started to mix up – to an absurd degree – two words: you and I. And I know that's from constantly overthinking the same thing, and maybe it would do me good to go out and work in the garden or head to the river and take a dip, and not always get bogged down with the same things. But I don't know how to do anything else.

I'll tell you that I saw the wolf again today, lying in the garden, tranquil. He gleamed silvery beneath the moonlight that spotlit the grass. The grass appeared softer than ever, and it seemed, at the same time, like a cover of shiny pins scattered over the garden. His eyes were glass and I saw myself, convex, in their irises: the immense head and the long, curved body. And it wasn't alone there: it was accompanied by a lamb, fluffy and round, resting its head on the wolf's belly. There are lambs in the forest, Boris, they must've escaped from some farm and made their way here. The wolf stuck out its tongue and dragged

111

it over the lamb's forehead, wiping its eyes and cleaning the sleep from them, then tracing its ears and an empty sound was heard when he stuck it inside them. And then the wolf closed its eyes and did the same thing to the other ear.

The lamb breathed slowly, its tummy grew and shrank, at a pace that remained stable for the hours I watched them. The wolf only sometimes moved, and the lamb understood it, because it would get up first and the wolf curled around in three or four circles, searching for its tail before lying down again. The lamb, meanwhile, watched it impassively and, when the wolf had lain down once more, it sank back into its chest; all as if saying: sign my death with your teeth.

I'll write more tomorrow. I think of you, Boris. (Your name wanted you, and you chose it!)

I turn on the light. Atop the table, dust. I use the cloak of darkness to write to Boris and tell him how I saw the wolf and the lamb embracing: how they licked each other and looked into each other's eyes, and each recognised the other's gaze. How they each knew the other's name. He doesn't know that it is a lie, that I made it all up. It wasn't a wolf, it wasn't even the shadow of a wolf; I just wanted to talk about him and me. About how I love him. I already want to leave, as he promised me long ago.

My mother shouts, warning me that – contrary to all expectations – the last tanks are leaving. We go up to her bedroom and from there, at the window, we see them in a row, armoured and thick. They drag past the last few houses like caterpillars but leave no visible trace: no slime wizening on the asphalt, just a sensation of wideness between our lungs. We celebrate with shouts unheard, that the row of tanks is heading off to some uncertain place, beyond the forest and the city. We look at the sky and we give thanks in silence, then we look at the earth and we say goodbye to them with still hands. The departure is like ripping off a scab. As we lose sight of the final tank, we scratch at it furiously until blood streams down our legs. If only it would come back like that, with that potency, the life from before. Mother cried and I know it wasn't just out of joy, that she was also sad to say such a vacant goodbye to the man with the shaved head who she thought was leaving, without concern for her or their memories. I smile, observing her out of the corner of my eye, happily. We haven't learned much, over this time; we haven't understood anything either. Who will bring us letters now?

II

Hell is where we're bound.

MARINA TSVETAEVA

HOOK

I put the photographs back in the envelope and I stored it in my pocket. Maybe so it could offer me an intimate and cosy view of what was foreign to me, in moments of longing (like the one of a row of horses, which I'd never seen before, eating quietly; or the one of the sheep running down the road, with no clear direction); maybe it could offer me an exotic and distant view of what was familiar to me, in moments of doubt (the derelict gardens; my body standing atop a rock, looking up at the sky; the trees that fall in the forest when the wind picks up). Flouting people's wishes, Boris had taken those photos, and I carried them with me because it meant that, at the same time, I was conveying a piece of unfinished biography. And because a photo always implies that another photo will follow it, and then another, and yet another; and that was what I needed to repeat to myself: that nothing was ending. Out of vanity, sentimentality or to not forget my hatred: I don't know whether I wanted to hold on to them out of fear of forgetting or to keep the rage from dissipating. If each of those photographs was a story, their accumulation was the closest to the experience of memory, a story with no end. Every once in a while, I would sink my hands into my pocket and graze them with my fingers. These are some of them:

FLIGHT

A patch of ceiling fell on me. A fragment of clear sky that detached, damp and soft, from this old apartment filled with leaks, caving in and onto my face, with very fine dust and broken plaster on the bed. I wake up not knowing where I am, disorientated from a blow that feels like the closest thing to hurling myself against a wall, with no hands. Boris wakes up from the scream, and tells me to be quiet, asks why I was shouting like that. I make coffee for us both while he goes back to sleep. From the window, at this height, you can see the part of the hill they hollowed out, now blending in with the rest, yet a trace remains: a patch devoid of the thick-trunked trees and the green boughs you can see from my mother's house. A city that is nothing. I'm surrounded by tall buildings, covered in glass, looking at and pointing at each other, accusing each other, and with cracks, broken mirrors that multiply the other mirrors and project the light to this window of ours. As if the buildings were only there to illuminate us, to nourish our animal passion now rooted in the city. The air that screams. A city that is nowhere.

MURMUR

Everyone wants to be happy. Everyone wants to be happy. Everyone wants to be happy. And there are those who say it into the mirror, holding their own gaze, and there are those who perhaps cross their fingers so that nothing bad will happen and pray to ward off all sadness. I couldn't stop running that over in my mind, like a futile mantra to keep me from putting the bag down on the ground, turning around and going back home. Inside the bag I'd put a pair of socks, the few T-shirts I owned, my dad's jack knife and a ring my mother had given me when I was young. The green was already far away, the dark green, black green, white fog green and grey green of night turning to dawn, and yellow green of the first light of day beginning to emerge. And I repeated all that to myself, and sometimes there was no need to repeat it because I felt confident like a migrating bird, fearless, with no nostalgia, no grief, nothing, because what the bird does is deeply instinctual, fleeing. And in other moments I had to repeat it again, and I said to myself, 'Everyone wants to be happy.' Eventually there was no need, I just acted on a primitive and animal conviction that compelled me to another place, without looking back, with another green to tint it all.

Boris drinks the coffee as if distracted by a loftier idea, and I look at him, just out of bed. His hair like wires conducting electricity. I'm not used to seeing him like that, half asleep, or to lying with him at night and not sleeping alone; but I like going to bed with someone, holding him, and then letting him go, measuring the distance that separates us in the darkness, and knowing that there's someone besides me in the room. I would like to explain to him, in words, what is going on with me inside, in a whisper, but it is also enough for me to look at him and listen as he explains our next steps. He puts down his mug and leans towards the window; I follow him. Before us is this desolate void that contains us, that we once called civilisation: now emptied of other people. Memories, deep down, are no different from a city. And, occasionally, I don't know if I miss the garden, the river, the animals, the boards, the cow and Vita's sister stroking it, the dark and green view from the windows, the old houses crumbling . . . no, no, that is a lie. Lies.

INVASION

I also kept track of how much of the road we'd already travelled, and I promised myself that, once we'd passed the halfway point, I wouldn't allow myself any doubts, or vacillations, or longing. The road grew smaller and then broadened, I could only see two metres in front of me – now narrower, now wider – and I amused myself by tracking the mutating width with my gaze. And meanwhile I ruminated that if years ago, with my dad alive, the houses well painted, the city full and Vita's sister locked up at home, that if years ago they'd told me that I would find myself like this, wandering in the night, I would've thought my brain had been invaded by an army of tiny aliens intent on making life more difficult for me. And that these microscopic extra-terrestrials, with nearly invisible pins, were like a spider in my skull devouring my nerve centres, kicking my brain to make me think sad lonely crazy stuff. Such as that, one night many years from now, I will find myself in a deserted city going to an apartment whose location I can't recall; and that the city will offer itself up to me naked and dead. And I lifted my head and there were hundreds of skyscrapers in front of me, and I didn't know where I was or where I should start looking.

After the coffee and gathering our belongings, bags hanging from my back and arms, I follow him and we leave the apartment, the building and the city behind. We go to the top of the hill and, then, there is that same view that I'd had with my mother, years ago, as we watched them burying earth within the earth. The same view I'd had not that many weeks earlier, at the peak of the little hill, overlooking the city and the houses on the other side. And north of there, the mountains, and some mines eviscerating them, as if they'd overtaken the lives of those tall and pointed hills. From here, with Boris by my side, one horizon is a gleaming, bluish and machinic steppe; and the other an uncontrolled savagery of green. Where to begin? If we are silent and open our eyes wide, we can hear the sound hiding beneath the silence of the dozing city and the beating hearts of the small animals slipping through the forest undergrowth. Luckily, most of the things that we can see from here will survive us. And then we take the path down, past where the wolf devoured the man with the shaved head. Not a trace. I don't tell Boris anything and we keep heading down until we reach my garden gate.

VOICE

I knocked on a door. No response. I knocked on another door. No response. I knocked on another door. No response. I knocked on another door. No response. I left that block of apartments, because, little by little, I was starting to convince myself that I'd made a mistake, and I went into the one beside it. All the skyscrapers were open, their entrances either broken or missing. I went up to the third floor and again tried each of the apartments. No response. No response. And, at the third door, no response, but a soft creak after the knocking, someone getting up out of a chair. Then, some extremely slow footsteps. Then, the carnal murmur of two arms moving and the metallic sound of keys jangling. 'It's me, Boris.' Then, a gust of wind collapsed the stillness, breaking that slow, rehearsed tension. Finally, the door opening, scraping the rough, dirty floor, and Boris's face out of joint, asking me what the fuck I was doing there.

We enter through the garden, leaping over the rusty gate. The vegetable plot is dry. The hens aren't there, or the pig, only the cow, tranquil. The furrows are undone and the stalks, dark and dehydrated, stretch up out of them. A green glaze covers the pond, like a veil, and on the surface there are water striders that move agilely, and tadpoles: that pool of hot water like the origin of the world. Boris follows me: it's been a while since he's seen this garden and I imagine he hardly recognises it, so abandoned. A small fox, when it sees us, runs towards the main road, crossing the tiled path that surrounds the house. I lift my head from the water, where I see myself reflected. The weeds reach our calves. Flies throng around our arms. The mosquito screen is open and the wind bangs it against the door, with thuds that make the wood creak. With each bang it seems the house is about to collapse, leaving a void in this sad little place of piled-up hovels. When I step on the rickety stairs, I can hear my mother ordering me: 'Don't jump, you'll break them,' and I, quite young, jumping with serious eyes and holding her gaze, and her coming over, slowly, and me jumping even harder: her advancing with each step, me jumping more and more determined.

DEBT

He told me, first of all, that we'd go by the house, because it was no good fleeing without saying anything and that if you have a mother, you say goodbye to her when you're leaving forever. I couldn't have imagined that crossing the forest, the hill and the ghost city and then showing up at his apartment would mean having to leave three weeks later. I followed Boris the way I'd followed, years earlier, those who called me bent and depraved; the way I'd accommodated them. Then, completely off the rails, I'd turned myself into their bullseye, into their bed, into the perfect prey, a little plucked bird before them, with thin skin. Without victimhood or hardship: I was the one who handed myself over, a burning torch in one hand, but I never dared throw it at them, and a case of knives in the other, which I offered to them, docile. He said: 'First, we'll go by your house.' And I followed him. I believed in him, the way I believed in the forest, in my dad's death, in my vegetable plot and in the rat room. Where? He said: 'First, we'll go by your house.' I followed him.

The house gives off a scent I can't identify. The sunroom is empty: splattered with white, the wicker chairs, the worn cushions, the red window frames. The ceramic figurine of a lioness on the table, with her two front paws raised, roaring, looks at me with glass eyes, neck turning. I rub my eyes to meet her gaze clearly and when I focus on her again her head is in place, immobile. Along her back there's a long, regular crack; in the open slit are accumulated papers and envelopes. I read my mother's handwriting, the verticality of the lines she writes for the letters that go up and down. The warmth of the space has petrified the furniture. The blinds are lowered, and blades of light enter through the tiny rectangles. In the dining room there are scattered grains of maize, that concentrated brightness. I fold the blanket that's on the sofa, I fluff up the cushions. I ask Boris to raise the blinds. Dust covers the junk lightly: a new, young dust that has settled like a carpet over recent days. I run my fingertip over the table and pick up ash. An innocent dust. As if life still breathed in the house that, suddenly, felt distant to me. And the dust makes it seem even more alive, and the house exhales. With each exhalation, it releases a sigh that accumulates slowly on top of the things. But this house no longer yearns: as if it were waiting for me.

PUNCH

Hard nipples crest beneath her clothes. The frozen peaks of two very high, unfamiliar snowy mountains: not the tip of our small hill but more like the top of a craggy range six thousand metres high, with pieces of ice melting and detaching from the rock. They were glimpsed, pointy, beneath the white blouse and still seemed colder and harder, those peaks. Perhaps I saw it that way because she was cold: she had cold cheeks, cold arms, cold eyelids. I imagined a person who had stretched out atop the snow and let themself be buried by the flakes that kept raining down. And it was hot, in that old room of Vita's: entering her house was like transferring our existence to another distant, old life. With no doors, just rooms separated by blankets hanging from the walls. With no beds, she slept on bundles of hay covered with thick esparto sheets. With no burners, so she cooked over the fire she lit every morning and snuffed out every night before sleep. It was hot. The heat made me woozy. And it was her cold, the cold that emanated from her horizontal body, that solidified her nipples, two diamonds scraping the fabric, wanting to break free from the flesh, tear the clothes and escape to the heavens. It wasn't the bedroom that was cold, it was Mum, who'd been lying dead for days.

We leave the dining room and see the dark stairs: an extremely long passage leading upwards. I don't want to climb them: the world was outside. We pass through the hallway and I open the door: tall weeds, beyond the porch, and large vine-leaves from unfamiliar plants, with small flowers, savage vegetation. Some yellow, some white, some purple. The fox again slips through the bushes. On the porch is my mother's chair, where she waited for my dad to arrive over so many years – evenings and evenings on the same porch: an image that doesn't erode with time – and later she waited for the man with the shaved head, who never came back. The forest had eaten him and all that was left of that adventure, which warms me as I recall it, was the dried-out, flayed rope. We go out onto the street. The asphalt burns. Vita comes out of her house, looks at me with a strange expression and, when she sees Boris coming up behind me, another expression etches her face, a suspicious one. 'Come here!' she shouts.

STRANGER

I was thinking: 'Mother died today. Or yesterday, maybe, I don't know.' Vita told me: 'Your mother died.' Obviously that doesn't mean anything. I thought: 'Maybe it was yesterday. Or maybe it was today.' It was hot. She was cold. Lying on a cot in Vita's house. I touched her cheeks, her eyelids. They were cold and blue. Her face was a plastered white, painted with a pale lilacness on the lips, a little blueness on the lids, a little greyness below the eyes. A mannequin. I tried to think of the last time she'd seen me. I didn't know. I tried to think of the last time I saw her. I didn't know. I invented a moment. I transferred a memory and I turned it into a final meeting: her, in the garden, pulling weeds. No. Too long ago. But when had I seen her, after that? I didn't know. First night of mourning? Second night of mourning? Third night of mourning? I didn't know. Fourth night of mourning? I didn't know. She was still whole. 'My mother didn't die today. She's been dead for days. Maybe yesterday. Or the day before yesterday, I don't know. Or maybe a week ago. She did not die today.' The fresh dust in the house. Such tall weeds in the garden. 'Mum didn't die yesterday. Maybe a week ago. Or maybe two. I don't know.' Vita told me: 'Your mother died. That's how it is. Come in. What in the world are you doing with him? She's inside. Come in.' She lay stretched out behind the hanging blanket, which served as a door. Mum. Vita turned to me: 'Here, this is for you.'

SON   I have the right to say things:

I was born in silence, not crying out
I lived in silence   wherever I went, I spoke the wrong way
first, where I was born, <u>there</u>,
they told me 'shut up, that's not how you should speak'
they corrected my words, they corrected my sentences
they said 'no, not insults, not curses,
don't speak to adults like that'
I told them at least I speak my mother tongue
YOUR tongue
I tricked them   to make them happy:
I told them words I didn't understand

later, once I was <u>here</u>, they told me
'shut up, you talk too much like them'
and they pointed their fingers beyond the mountains
they would say
'that word is like this, that doesn't mean anything here'
they would say
'hide that hellish accent'
they would say
'I'm telling you this because I want the best for you'
I tricked them   to make them happy:
I told them words I didn't understand

when you read this, I'll have died in silence

133

I lived my whole life waiting for ~~a god~~ a miracle
I don't know how to say much to you   just in case:
don't wait for it, it won't come
memories are lonely bullets in the night
but they can also be light against the shadows
I grew up without thinking that I had to save
everything I was experiencing
later, without memories, somehow I stopped living
I tried to do things, not to kill time: I wanted to do them
I would say 'I believe in this, I want to do this'
I WOULD DO IT
I tried to do it
and I did them while forgetting the rest:
~~I would forget   forget forget~~

the legacy of my language: pain
grow up speaking because they tell you no,
and no, and no, and no
flee all that, later, and yearn for the pain   yearn for what?
~~to~~ my parents, ~~I would say~~:
you handed down your legacy of pain
in silence   I would hide behind the words I didn't say
from the silence I listened to the indifference
with which the adults spoke of indifferent things
I learned to see pretending I was listening
I saw them   I didn't listen

at home   make a home and live inside it
my home   your father's home
for years I've seen how the fruits open in the garden
how they rot and from them grew a new tree

134

and, in it, another fruit
another fruit that again fell cloying sweet and opened,
and from it grew a new tree
and the years passed like that
the snow the sun more snow more sun
~~the sun the snow more sun more snow~~
my life has been   a long wait
don't ever wait so long the way I did
I waited many years and nothing happened
always the same porch
always the same forest
now green, now yellow, now brown, now nothing
waiting my whole life for a man
    the same: waiting my whole life for an idea
    the same: waiting my whole life for   what?

I was born far from here
I didn't know that being born far from here
meant 'waiting' always
I was born, I left and I loved
I didn't know, then, that I was wrong
suddenly: make a home and live inside it
unlike what they say, mistakes are not the portal to discovery
being wrong is an abandonment
being right is an abandonment

in silence I understood that my error
would follow me forever
that if I was wrong, maybe the mistake <u>was me</u>

[illegible sentences here]

135

The flames gleam in his eyes and the glow moves over his face. I can feel my cheeks baking hot, my eyes throb cold, and the gleam must also be moving in them. Beneath the fire, the wood screams. The fox, from the other side, half hidden, observes us curiously. I see the red, orange colours, and the white and blue and lilac tips in Boris's gaze. The wood screams and I hear a beam collapsing and some furniture bursting: the hinge of a door, the marrow of a bookshelf, the explosion of an old glass pane. Boris places a hand on my shoulder, in the most intimate gesture of holding me, and tells me that everything will be okay. For him, a hug. For me, a pat with the palm of his hand sustained through time, extending the farewell caress. And that is why, when he places his hand on me and my mother's house – now my house? – burns like a forest, I believe that maybe everything will indeed be alright. A flare-up pierces the attic and emerges furious through the ceiling. With the gusts of wind, the fire irons my forehead, singes my cheekbones. The wind magnifies the flames and the wood shrieks even more. If this house is memory – now mine? – and every wooden floorboard a recollection, we are demolishing it all ruthlessly. It seems too easy to say, but I feel the fire inside me.

Boris starts the car. Both of us in silence. The sound of the engine hypnotising us. We drive away from the dead end, that corner of the world, with the same self-doubt as a mother who leaves her son sleeping in bed, in his room, and has the whole night ahead of her, just as dark and unfathomable. Vita told me that my mother died peacefully. That for a few days she hadn't seen her leave the house and she already knew. In bed, like a hot puppy. And that she had left that long, long letter, on the bedside table, for them to find, but that she had written it a while back: there were corrections, different inks, and some big letters, and then some smaller ones, and then big ones again. Boris follows a road, I don't know where it leads. Through the rear-view mirror we see the smoke, like a warning that we should not return. I grip the letter with rigid fingers, as if there were no safer place in the world for it to be, because my mother says more things in it than she said over those last months. Had she been writing it during those days when I saw her shuffling around the garden and resting in the chair? Why hadn't she explained it to me then? I shout: 'Mother!' and Boris tells me that she can't hear me. And I turn, then, to look her in the eyes and plead with her but she remains stretched out on the back seat, bumping with the motion of the car. My dad died first, yes, but I still don't understand death, and it's the first time my mother has died. And the problems have piled up on me, even more difficult and big and unfeasible: what had been a desire – fleeing – now becomes an obligation – burying. How to learn to live again, I wonder.

[two illegible sentences here]

you left me   a scar
my belly from top to bottom and a line
there is never a day I don't think about you
in front of the mirror
my hand beneath my clothes
the texture like a hill range in the middle of my body
as if you didn't want to be born   nestled tight
and a long slice to evict you
you didn't cry
I picked you up in my arms and I said   what's this?
why doesn't he cry? shouldn't he   cry?

[more parts that can't be read]
with you   a piece of the world that's ending
a whole world
I wanted you to cry, for you to say no to the world
NO NO NO
no no
you didn't cry   but I picked you up in my arms and I cried
because I could already sense that a piece of the world
was ending for me
a whole world
I wished you'd stayed there inside
that they hadn't evicted you
that they'd let me carry you without taking you out

139

that they hadn't cut me open from one end to the other
and that if you came out, if you decided to come out,
you would cry   but no
but it was me who cried

you grew up
I didn't want to leave you what they'd left me with: pain
I wanted to give you life   how?? as you grew
every day I rubbed the scar
in front of the mirror   my hand beneath my clothes
the texture of bark on my belly
I thought what will I leave him,
~~what will I leave him, what will I leave him~~
nothing   I couldn't leave you a thing

I couldn't leave you a thing, even if I wanted to
the vegetable plot, the animals, this house in ruins   but no
you have to burn it   burn it
not a trace of the walls, the furniture, the ceiling
and you   you have to leave
    first: because you can't stay here
    second: because I don't want to stay here
not in this house   not in this garden
all I ask of you   bury me far away   from here

What if we come up against, on the road, more coiled razor wire, not rusted, not collapsing but with tall spikes? Boris keeps driving. A few hours earlier we'd filled the tank with old demijohns of petrol that she stored beneath a sticky old rag. I watched him, sitting on the bonnet, like you watch the surgeon slicing open your body without anaesthesia. I sensed the sweet caramel scent of the liquid and the sound of emptiness as it fell inside the metal. The demijohn trembled in his hands. Like my hand trembled when I left the house behind and approached him. Two unknown spaces, his and mine. And how stupid I was, believing that we could leave there on foot, walking through the days along endless paths. He put down one demijohn and picked up another. He tossed the one he'd emptied onto the ground, with a bang, not setting it down carefully. As if he were chain smoking and anxiously tossing the butts. Looking at Boris, I saw my blurred reflection: the car. He'd wanted to come by the house for the car. And I could feel the brush of the razor wire around me, curling hairs, ripping skin, as if Boris encircled me and I could not escape him. But what I also find incomprehensible is watching him drive, serious, and thinking that I want to share with him all the things in the world that can be shared in all the places and in all the ways possible.

EPICENTRE

We drove for days in a straight line. The landscape shifted through the windows. We went through vast fields filled with rows of fruit trees and uniformed women who gathered the fruits: they wore their hair pulled back in a net. Then Boris told me that we had left the affected zone, but there were hardly any people. A few houses beside the road, where solitary men sold petrol to the few cars that passed by. No one spoke. No one asked questions. You gave them coins and they filled the tank. Sometimes they told us that the banknotes were too old and if we wanted petrol we had to give them food or do what they ordered us to. That was how we spent the first six days, driving away from the abundant smoke of the house and from the narrow street and from the wide forest and from what we'd lived through, which remained there forever. You could no longer see the mountains on the horizon. We lost sight of them on the first day of our journey. While Boris drove, I asked him to repeat what would happen, when it was all over. And despite not knowing anything about what awaited us, we had gradually configured a story that appeased us. Boris would recite: 'We'll live by the sea. We'll live in a place where we'll see the waves, the sand, the rocks. We'll have a stretch of land and we'll never work. Except in our vegetable plot. We'll have money. And rabbits of every colour. We'll plant wisteria, roses, camellias, geraniums and lindens. All the trees and plants that can't survive the winter or the mountain snow. They'll take root and sustain us from below. The mornings will stretch long, beneath the sun, and the afternoons will be tranquil. We'll swim in the sea and we'll sleep, the wind will dry us off and it won't be cold.' I would listen to him, closing my eyes, squeezing my hands together, as if my knees were on a wooden pew and his voice was the homily. And that smell, of incense and humidity, of abandoned church, was now the decaying flesh of my mother.

Boris asks: 'Here is fine, right?' I glance back at her after I saw a sad hole beside the hard shoulder of the road, in the middle of an infinite dry plain. Here Boris saw the ideal place to get rid of her, once and for all, an opportunity to travel lighter and use less petrol. My mother had said no, not there, not on that steppe, where every point is interchangeable with every other point. Burying is putting someone in a place that's not just any old place. Not only in case you go looking for it someday, but also so that the dead person feels that they are resting in a unique and definitive spot. And there are people who are more unique dead than alive, because then they find their place in the world to distinguish themselves from the rest. Others are buried by the side of the road or in mass graves covered with dirt, and dying is as grey as living had been. Even if life hadn't been grey at all, for them, but it had been for others. And, in the end, what others say about you is what you are, whether you like it or not. I say to Boris: 'Let's keep going.'

TOMBS

We rise at dawn with the sky damp, no frost, because the cold is in the frozen air that slices our unprotected faces and hands, and hasn't yet accumulated on the ground. The needle on the gauge above the steering wheel was stuck on the red light. We had to say yes, we need the petrol. The first dusk was also freezing and caught us by surprise: when we arrived with the car and I got up to buy the two demijohns, the dryness of the steppe didn't seem to suggest that the nights would be glacial and wet. We know that we are far from home: there, when it's cold it's cold, but when it's hot it's hot. Here, when the sun sets and shares sky with the moon, someone splatters the sky with a freezing vapour that gets into your bones and freezes them, so that a little tap could break them. And as we start to gather fruit in the dawn, I cross my fingers that I won't fall and break an arm or a leg, they are so rigid. The farm is immense. There are animals in some old stables, too, but most of the expanse is never-ending fields of robust and spiky fruit trees. To pick the fruit you have to break open the shells that make your fingers bleed and, once you've separated them, you have to extricate the fruit that clings to stalks covered in thorns. To loosen it, you have to hold up the small branch and your fingertips bleed. They don't give us any gloves. No one says anything. Some long dogs with pointy ears, muscular thighs and extremely wide chests watch over us. There are twenty or thirty of them. There are also some men who aim weapons at us. I pluck a fruit. When it falls into the basket it makes a dull thud.

GAME

The man told me that they were too old, the banknotes, that they weren't good any more. You could deduce, from his accent, that he'd learned our language by speaking it, repeating the same words over and over, like a song. Best I could, I explained that we needed the petrol to keep on going. 'Mother,' I was thinking, 'Mother'. He looked at me without listening. He had a bulbous face with two greasy cheeks. He was fat and crossed his hairy arms in front of me. I was thinking, 'Mother.' He repeated: 'Yes or no?' As I said yes, and in the single moment when 'yes' could be said, I saw the colours of the germs inside my mother, their super-thin and curly tube shapes, the overflowing capsules, their walls surrounded by spikes, the gelatinous membranes propelled by long flagella. Mother. All of that inside her and in my eyes, in front of a stranger, inside a farm, in a valley who knows where, between obscure hills, in a zone of foreign language.

Boris, three trees over. I look at him. I think about Mum, stretched out in the car, and us stuck here for days now. Over a couple of demijohns of petrol. The coiled razor wire on the horizon levitates above his head, a crown of thorns. The true crown of thorns. The boy beside me has a coarse and square face, but hides friendly lips beneath his nose, as he gathers fruit with surprising agility. I've been noticing him for some days. He is very young, no more than a couple of years older than us. I take a risk and ask him how long he's been here. 'Shut up.' One of the dogs barks at us. We continue picking fruit and gathering it in the round plastic baskets that drip with blood. He searches me out with his eyes: 'Two years,' moving his lips without projecting his voice. He speaks our language. He understands us. I keep looking at him: 'Did you come alone?' and he replies: 'No, I was heading north from the mountains with my brother.' He points him out, a few trees over. I tell him: 'We come from there too,' and I look at Boris, who stands out from the mass of other men with his bronzed skin. His eyes cloud over. 'My name is Me,' he says. I confess to him that we want to leave, but that the man had ordered us to stay a few days more. 'You won't make it out of here.' Then, silence. And we keep gathering fruit.

HUMP

First he showed us the room. 'You will sleep here.' We followed him outside. The horizon opened onto a stained desert. The earth was golden and there were hundreds of trees with old, rough trunks covered in spikes. An army of men was gathering the fruit. Animals on the plain. Each tree, a needle. Animals who had forgotten their names but didn't forgive, a rage inside that you could see in their eyes and by the way they moved their arms and grabbed the stalks, and by how they wiped their bloodied fingers on their clothes. Each man, a seed on the steppe from which nothing grew. I was convinced that those trees had long roots that drank the water deep below. He approached a nearby tree and touched a stalk without grabbing it. He pointed to a hard brownish ball like a nut. 'Inside there is the fruit you have to harvest.' He gave us a couple of baskets. The blood of the men, when it fell to the ground, turned the sand into mud. The defenceless part of me said yes. Each mouth, a wound. Without having tried it, I had already learned to extract the fruit and aim it into the round basket. I was thinking, Mother. We began to work. The afternoon light gleamed on the shells, the spikes and the copper earth, and the landscape glowed like a gold ingot.

I keep watching Boris from a distance, with Me at my side. In the background, murmurs in the other language are audible. The dogs bark and bare their teeth when the murmur grows. The car, my mother, the seats. I say to Me: 'We'll escape from here in three nights.' He replies: 'Impossible.' The sun shines through the spikes in the trees: in each one, a star. I was hopeful we could flee. And also full of terror for the longer term: losing it all forever. Losing what? Me points out a man who is harvesting the fleshy spheres with one hand. 'They cut off his other hand when he tried to leave.' In front of everyone: they gathered them in a circle, planted him in the centre and they lopped his hand off with a hatchet. A very clean slice. And fed it to the dogs. I imagine Me's face, with his long arms around his brother; and, in the background, the murmur of the half-comprehensible language. The face of the man, watching as the dogs gnawed on his severed hand. His live flesh devoured. How can a life be welcomed inside another life? How can a language inside another language be understood? 'There is a place, at the far end of the field, where they throw the dead. They say there's no current there and that you can jump over the wall. But getting there is impossible.' I repeat: 'We will escape in three nights. Show us the place.' Me grows silent. He continues gathering fruit more quickly now, and grits his teeth – I could hear them grinding, nervous – and drops of blood drip onto his arm that he doesn't wipe off. He throws a handful hard into the basket. He looks at me and moves his lips again, with no voice: 'We'll go with you.'

STABLE

Minutes of silence until the drowsiness caught up to them. All the men asleep on cots, their faces suddenly calm, as if the alcohol they gave them at night, before bed, had undone their fatigue. We must have been twenty men. I'd lost count of the days we'd spent there. Beside me, Me breathed roughly, against the rhythm of the rest. Boris and I were forced to sleep in separate rooms. Me and his brother too. A glimmer illuminated us. And from the bed, I saw the contours of the slender men, half naked and covered with wool blankets, like cows that breathe deeply without fear. As if sedated. And they seemed like cows because of the pointy bones that stuck out on their shoulders, like the cow we used to have in the garden, that the sister with the weird face always groped. I thought that Me breathed like I did, with a different rhythm, with momentum. I got up and stretched out on his cot, on my side. He turned and in a very low voice asked me if I couldn't sleep either. His voice didn't break the night's calm. His eyes burned and, in his face, there was no sign of tiredness. Yet I, before him, did feel my weaknesses: my exhausted body, the tedium that cradled my soul, and a familiar rawness in each thing I thought about. Maybe I needed to get used to it, I don't know, or maybe I needed this company.

FIELD

During the shared time before sleep, in his bed, Me told me about a stretch of the mountains I had never seen. The place where he and his brother came from. He said that, from the other side, they weren't dark or pointed: they were round and had trees that grew at impossible angles, and goats with incredibly long horns that defied the heights. He said that he remembered them green, and with life, and with light. Not me, I could only think of them as grey, craggy and cloud-covered. He also told me about the houses where they lived, and suddenly my world expanded, and I imagined them from a bird's perspective, as if I were an eagle flying over them, and I was telling myself that they were large, and tall, and with tidy gardens and roofs bursting with sunshine. From the sky I drew rows of houses like the blue house, but in different colours and shapes, and with people inside who weren't sad like the rich people on my street were. How terribly hard it was to understand that all that was on the other side of the rock wall. And how the mountains didn't matter when it all happened, when everyone on the other side was forced to flee their homes as well. And how wild is it, I thought, that we speak the same language, despite the distance. As if it were a spilled vase that had splattered drops of water over different places. And before I fell completely asleep, I even thought how stories, like this one that Me was explaining, can always be rewritten. But not memories. And the drowsiness, of course, the drowsiness caught up to us just like it had the rest.

153

We walk through the darkness, avoiding the cots, confident that Boris and Me's brother are waiting for us. The men sleep with slack faces and some empty bottles still clasped in their hands, and there are more bottles on the floor. When the door opens, a silvery glow enters the bedroom. Outside, the moon is almost full. Between some trees we can make out two silhouettes. We approach them. Me says: 'Follow me.' His brother greets us with an attentive gaze and trembling lips. The moon reflects on the blade of the knife Me carries in his hand. He asks us, as we stealthily walk towards the far end: 'Do you know what they do with the fruit?' He continues: 'They say they make drugs for those who fled the mountains and the surrounding cities, when it all happened.' We keep walking, passing through the shadows. We can already make out a wall at the far end when a light is aimed at us. We start running, dodging it. Fast. Faster. I hear the whistle of a bullet. We run even faster. Then, the sound of a shot. I turn and don't see Boris. Another shot. We continue on, running without stopping. The light following us, as if god were pointing at us from the sky. I run. We change direction, through the trees. The light follows. I run. I had never run that much before. I follow the figure in front of me. I assumed it was Me. I run. The sharp branches of the trees tearing my skin. The earth breathing, beneath my feet. I run. The light loses us among the trees. We reach the wall. And I only see two profiles.

154

SHOT

Eleven years. I ran. I had never run that much. A thrown rock. Fast. Faster. I looked back, to see how far away they were. Another rock. I ran. They shouted: 'Run, skeleton!' They shouted: 'Doesn't matter if you run!' On the horizon, I saw my house and the forest. I was thinking, 'Mother.' They shouted: 'You can go to the forest, it makes no difference, we'll shove a huge stick up your asses!' I ran. I was afraid of slipping on the leaves that carpeted the ground. The hill: a rotting plum, yellow and orange and brownish. I ran. Just as a blind person says that for him the colours are like god, mysterious, my desire for that racing melted, and from all that running I sensed that my desire wasn't abstract but concrete: running forever, having faith, a lot of faith, like the faith of the blind man who says 'red' and says 'blue' and says 'green' and flees, flees forever. And also that the habit doesn't assuage the suffering but that, from so much repetition, it makes one used to running, and running even more. Like my mother, who had worked so long at the Factory that she had calloused fingertips and could grab oven trays without gloves. But the calloused stayed hard, even though they no longer burned. And my legs were tired too. And my entire spirit, my soul, was also surrendering, to the others. I ran. I saw the house, not far off. I was thinking, 'Mother.'

I see Me's face. The glow puts him in high relief and his face looks more like the bark on a tree than the face of a boy: it defines his aquiline nose, his deep eye sockets, his narrow jaw and sharp chin. In black and white. As if sprayed by a platinum aerosol. I look at the other shadow: Boris. My chest grows, seeing him there and knowing that he wasn't touched by the shot. Me holds the knife with one hand, trying to hold back his exhalations with the other on his belly. From where we ran, the round yellow light approaches, searching for us. Some dogs bark. A torrent of tears rushes through me: I feel grief and joy at the same time, because Boris is with me but Me has lost his brother in just a few seconds; the light draws near and the useless knife he holds between his fingers makes our situation even more ridiculous. The end is slowly being written, with the force of the suspense in our three bodies that have slowly become flaccid, fragile as insects who have tender green bones. In that moment, I find Boris and Me so vulnerable, with innocent faces and still vibrant eyes: they are boys. Me says: 'Jump here,' and he points to a heap of sand beside an enormous hollow. It smells of deep well and dead animal. He hands me the knife and says: 'Don't lose it.' And he adds: 'Run, I'll say that it was just the two of us.' He is not like the rest of the men there: he draws near to love against the blinding light, towards his brother's fallen body, against life. Boris and I leap. I etch into my memory the name 'Me' and the rapt, trembling gaze of his brother.

On the other side of the wall, it smells different. We manage to leave the farm thanks to a hill of earth protruding from a mass grave. Men inside the earth. Earth inside the earth. The wall is extremely high; I fall face down. The earth, on this side, is thick and damp, grainy from when the worms turn it over and make big spongy balls with it. Thick and damp. I grab a handful. I squeeze it tightly. In my palm it feels hard, compact, like a handful of cement. How can a language inside another language be understood? I follow him, running. How can a life be welcomed inside another life? He heads towards the entrance to the farm. The door is open. He comes out a few seconds later with two demijohns and we run to find the car without looking back.

GOAL

Eleven years. The earth there was thick and damp, grainy, from the hens that pecked at it and turned it over and shat in it. Thick and damp. I heard them shout: 'Where are you!' I grabbed a handful. I squeezed it tightly. In my palm it felt hard, compact, like a handful of cement. They shouted: 'Where are you, cocksucker!' They shouted: 'The more you hide, the worse it's gonna be when we find you!' Inside it was dark. Like when I would lock myself in the room with the raw loaves. I had gone through the tiled passageway towards the back garden and hidden in the henhouse. Mother said I talked like the hens. Friends. Their voices and their beating wings: my voice and my moving hands and arms as I spoke. My swish, the others said. Cowards, I said. One of them approached the henhouse, and said to the rest: 'He must be in here,' and I heard the footsteps of the one approaching, he sliced the dried leaves with each step, and I held the pressed earth in my palm to throw into his eyes if he found me, or maybe just to endure the fear that gripped me. The wood on the henhouse gate cracked, where he was leaning, and another voice told him: 'What are you talking about, moron, he must have gone into the forest, that son of a bitch.' And they headed to the forest. I heard how their crunching footsteps grew increasingly far away and soft. How they jumped over the rusty gate. How their arms brushed their hips. How the trees' shade covered them. I released my fist: the dirt ball was dark brown with white and greyish flecks. And it came apart in my hands, and I saw that it was slipping through my fingers like the years sliding through my body. I stayed there until night fell, breathing slowly, as my mother had taught me to do in the trunk.

Opening the car, there's a stench of burned hair so piercing and hard you could cut it with the knife. I ask myself, what are we doing, Boris and I, in an old wreck, with my mother rotting to pieces, travelling through the night with two stolen demijohns of petrol. Violence: our birth certificate. Leaving behind an open wound with a radius of hundreds of kilometres. Violence: runs across the length of our skin. Our skin: seamless, just a terrible memory of years of isolation, of a splintered language, of an exile at home. As the days pass I have the sense that the revolution does not begin at home, no, it begins in the body. Our house: razor wire. The hill: a cemetery covered in green. Being born: wallowing in clay, dust and animal hair, in the dining room, and then being washed with rainwater. Speaking: reviving a dying language. Living: resisting the gusts of wind. And loving, for me: nearing a body equal to mine without knowing if it is poison or syrup. And it is always poison. Loving: sleeping with the door open, and my treasures on the table.

We drive in silence. When I try to speak, I remember Me's hand offering me the knife and I say nothing. From the road we've seen fields of fruit trees, the same ones that we'd harvested those nuts from, that are no longer just trees and they haunt us with their thorns, they uproot themselves and approach us, cornering us and stabbing us, one by one, until we bleed. I look at them, so pleasantly lined up, so anomalous, with robust trunks despite their young age, recently planted. And with so many fruits pouring off the branches, even on the thinner stalks. They are little dots on the horizon. Fields and fields of those trees. From a distance, each one is a thorn. When they were right in front of us, with our hands covered in wounds, each tree was thousands and thousands of thorns. That's how I imagine hell – not fiery, not red, not flaming, but thorny and twisted, filled with earth and earthworms, and tiny holes in the walls that let in air that's not hot or cold, that is thick and dense, like a cloud. Grottos that have roots for beams, vestiges for columns, and petroleum basins for seas without fish. That's my image of hell: earthy, covered in mud, sullied. And with those trees. I look at Boris. I see us trapped there, beneath an idea that we did not foresee. I think that, somehow, each of us helps the other live and, at some point, each of us will have to help the other die.

I give myself permission to kiss him, now that a few hours have passed and the farm is far in the distance. Prudence is sometimes intelligent because Boris turns his face to me, lowers his chin and calmly allows me. It is like resting for a while, like a slightly longer exhalation that, instead of going out, goes in towards my chest. But in that moment while we kiss, I feel the unexpected vigilance of a strange gaze, and I turn, frightened. The blanket has slipped and exposed my mother's face. She looks at us with closed but prying eyes, her cheeks hard and her forehead wide, accepting defeat; her dry tongue hanging out, expelled from her jaw, long like the tongue of that cow who used to wander through the garden. Beneath her lids, her eyes must be bloodshot, mapped with red lines, dry. With the same look of disgust of that afternoon many years ago. With the same wrinkles that formed around her eyes and the corners of her lips, when she saw us. With a similar disappointment in her cheekbones, when she understood what we were doing. I feel revealed, stripped bare. As if the kiss has disrobed her, lying there, or reminded her of what she'd discovered and told no one, except my dad, and that seethed alone inside her: a never-ending procession, an ulcer that opened up on the fleshy walls of her organs and pierced her from top to bottom. We've been apprehended by her spectral rictus that had survived guilt and judgement, and had left open, forever, the possibility that she could get up, frozen and white, and point at us, again, with her finger.

SMELLS

We hid among the trees, the ones behind the gate, beside the meadow. We did it instinctually, and at the same time we felt the warmth and the sweat of mischief, a hungry little worm that grew big, very big, and seduced our muscles when they tired from the effort and from that motion, so mechanical and so carnal. We passed the worm back and forth and when one of us felt our fire fading, the other was aflame, when one said: 'Stop, stop,' the other said: 'No, no'; and I looked up at the sky, curving my back, and I noticed the tree branches moving blurrily up and down, and all I asked was that they cover us from god, who is always watching, that they hide our innocent wickedness; Lord, we're just looking for that kernel of simple, natural pleasure, Lord, we aren't doing anything bad. It was ferocious, like the birth and death of the stars, an explosion amid all that green and the cow wandering around. A thick scent hovered, one I always yearned to grab, so I could put it in a little jar and smell it later, at night, in bed, unscrewing the lid and reliving it before going to sleep. The forest would grow in my brain, incredibly tall trees and lush boughs inside my mind. Another ceiling. And with my eyes closed I could again feel that river slipping in and up my nostrils, like salmon against the current, and flowing onto the muddy bank of my imaginary dwelling, with Boris's naked body banging into me both gently and hard from behind.

CORRESPONDENCES

For that was how I imagined heaven. Not cottony, not immense, not blue skies. In my mind's eye it was thick and carnal, filled with lush greenness and dry leaves on the ground, with scratches and caresses, with echoes that weren't songs, that were moans and bellows of men and animals. Passageways of natural light, like the shafts that entered through the breaks in the trees, with the smell of rain on fresh grass and bird shit, and ants carrying dead insects, and the indiscreet gaze of some sniffing creature. That was my image of heaven: that view, face down, with the clarity of that distorted perspective, every blade of grass as big as they seemed to me stretched out there. When I saw a shadow I turned my head to see my mother's face pale and disjointed. She wore a bewildered expression, as if she'd discovered herself, suddenly, faced with a phenomenon that she could not comprehend: the house in ruins, or the forest burned, or her son dead. With taut arms she was carrying a basket and a couple of bags filled with food: some pink, shiny cuts of meat; dark green leaves that emerged from the top. She also had a packet of chocolate powder, something she only bought once a year for a celebration at home in the evening. She would prepare a cake and we would dip it into our mugs of hot chocolate, and we would spend the months following evoking that evening. She was planted there, not saying a word or shifting her expression. Boris and I buttoning our pants and putting on our T-shirts, in front of her, like a punishment. Boris leaving through the garden, looking at the ground. I was left standing in front of my mother, thinking that the minimum probability of disaster never disappears. And that earth behind me and before me, where all the wicked things had happened to me, and where all the good things had happened too.

After a tunnel, the road climbs upwards and the sunlight hits us in the face with its rays. I wake up suddenly. On this side, the road extends like a thread and is surrounded by a forest of giant trees that are so tall you can't see where it ends: they reach right up to the sky and I swear some of the boughs go straight through the clouds. 'Boris, where do you think we'll end up? I mean, when we have to stop. I don't know, what should we do with my mother?' Boris doesn't know what to say, and neither do I. I suppose that's why he prefers not to respond and continues in silence. It is also true that having things to say is very difficult. He looks at me and lets out a weary smile that shows both worry and the lucid clarity of a safe way out. Those trees cover us, and at the same time they create the sensation that there is a lattice of very thick roots sustaining us from below. Like the steel that is mixed with cement in the foundations of houses, some incomprehensible ramifications support us within a natural order, both corrupted and fragile.

Boris's silence. My silence. Searching everywhere for the unconditional and all we find are things: words that gradually die within me and I no longer know how to say 'tree' or how to say 'sky' or how to say 'I don't like that' or 'I like that'. But with Boris by my side there are words that are unnecessary. For example, the word 'friendship' or the word 'love'. There's no need to say them, because they aren't words, those words, to me. Boris always repeats that he is just as free in a square as in a cell, just as free as he is now in this forest; that he will never say 'freedom' because freedom is not a word. And he always does that: Boris always says phrases he's read somewhere or another, and later confesses that he didn't invent those words himself, that he read them who knows where and can't remember now. He looks at me out of the corner of his eye, as I listen to him, and I find in his gaze something more atavistic than these trees, more animal than the wolves that run through the garden of my house. And I believe him, because I've told myself many times that he would never lie to me, not Boris. And, like that, the words thicken, and grow in our mouths, like rubber, guzzling our saliva. That's why, perhaps, I decide to keep quiet, to maintain the familiar silence reluctantly.

Beyond the windscreen and the rusty bonnet, in some deeper place along the road where the dashed lines disappear, we reach an end. The trees vanish and the forest is cut in a cross section. We approach slowly. Amid the trunks we feel protected. We speak. I know that sharing these secrets bonds us together and nestles our relationship deeper into a wider, stronger base. He talks to me about his parents. And I feel that pleasure burbling up, the pleasure I feel when Boris reveals a piece of his life. The orange glow of the sun slips through the botanic pillars. He speaks of that precise age when adults think that you only half understand the world but you understand it better than ever: when your hairs grow faster and you go to sleep with your muscles wounding you as they widen. They would organise meetings at home, his parents, and invite men and women over to suppers shrouded in silence. And they would speak in murmurs. They would tell Boris to stay in his room, but later, as he grew up, they would let him have supper with them and they would send him to bed when it was time to talk about serious things, as his father would say. Those men and women, he explains to me, made staggered arrivals throughout the afternoon. The first few right after they had lunch. Boris accepted the uncertainty as a mystery that he knew would later be revealed: always in a future that never came. From his room, he could hear voices: they linked together and then detached, and they mixed together in a never-ending swarm, the small apartment filled with hundreds of fish swimming in a fish tank. Since they couldn't open the window, a cloud of thick smoke grew in the dining room. And in the morning there were still traces of it, the thin puff of cloud that rests in the blue sky the day after a long night.

That morning his parents – under the smoky haze, the footprint of a banned word hanging in the air – sat him down in a chair in the kitchen. They stood before him, and they seemed older than ever. There are people who age suddenly and you don't know if it's your eyes that've changed how they see them, or if they have just surrendered over a matter of days. And he had them there rooted into the ground, with the haze surrounding them, speaking to him. And he must have nodded yes, with the confidence of a frightened child convinced that their parents' truth must be their truth. And he even tells me that they gave him an envelope that held some papers and some maps covered with instructions and markings, but then he quickly changes the subject, as if he's made a mistake.

We have reached the limit. One landscape ends and another begins. The sky can be seen again: the clouds like tree boughs, but white. Boris stops the car suddenly. My mother falls off the back seat, onto the muddy mats, her arm twisted like the inverted leg of a hen. It hurts me just to watch. Life has already escaped through her eyes but she is somehow present with her physicality, affirming her decomposed state in the world, revisiting her body in fits and starts, reminding us that she is here watching over us. Dead but alive. Our conversation enters her flesh; that light, beneath the trees, Boris's voice, calmer than ever before. Her arm brushes my back. I touch her skin and the texture of its surface is plastic – like when we found my granddad's dog in the garden, dead for days, and I sank my fingers into its flesh made of modelling clay. I pressed its muscles with my finger; they felt hard and when I pushed more, they shifted and then returned ever so gently into place. Boris tells me: 'Don't move.' Like a wax doll, that little dog was. Boris tells me: 'Turn gradually.' As if, having died, it was unflappable and there was nothing in the world that could change its shape. Boris tells me: 'Stop.' And now my mother's flesh is just like that: a simulacrum. I extend her arm and cover it with the blanket; I can't push her back up onto the seat from that twisted position. I sit up again and see it. Boris's braking, his jaw out of joint, the men aiming at us. Boris tells me: 'Stay still.'

PROMISE

His parents burning papers and photographs, gathering up clothes into garbage bags, tearing the pages out of some books. The mornings slid in, yellow with apricot light; the middays advanced, the sky like a river before reaching the ocean and the evenings stretched red and foggy. Boris seemed surprised by how the time moved: so still and imbalanced. The happiness of those days flared up and snuffed out without any explanation, because it merely consisted of keeping going, continuing on. He remained immersed in a situation that didn't belong to him, and that did not take him into consideration. He stretched out in bed and slept. The night filled him with nightmares: there were sounds, and a grey scaly snake that curled around him – it appeared with two heads, forked tongues, and then had three, and squeezed Boris tighter and tighter, then four heads, then five heads, and in the dream that moment was a whole day. He watched the colours pass: first yellow, then blue and then red. The scales brushed his skin, scraped it, and his flesh hardened, and the snakes were then arms, legs, fingers. And he got up, with the reptilian presence still in his muscles, and it was a clear day, the light was again apricot, like the other mornings, and like all those that were to come. He went out into the dining room and he found them there in the middle of the parlour, stretched out on the floor; his mother with her eyes open and his father with his hands on the knife stuck into his heart. Boris tried to pull it out but he stopped when he saw that, when he moved it, more blood came out of the wound. And he stayed there for hours, looking at them.

Behind their bodies is a high metallic fence crowned by rusty razor wire. I look to the left: nothing. I look to the right: nothing. Beyond the trees comes the desert. The men guarding the void. Aiming at us. There must be about ten of them. We can't see their faces. Some two hundred metres away there is a barracks with no door. And, beside it, a thick bar blocks access to the other side. They don't wear uniforms, instead they are covered by resistant shells that protect their muscles. Beneath is black chain mail that covers their bodies. Their heads are shielded by light helmets that mimic their skulls. Like ivy, the helmets grip their foreheads, cheekbones and chins and there are holes only for their eyes and their mouths. Their boots are soiled with fresh mud that hasn't yet turned to dirt. To the right a stream shimmers and the bank is muddy up to the border. They approach us, slowly, and their footsteps splash in the mire, as if they were walking on the moon, so slow, and each time they lift a leg they have to really pull, because their feet stick to the ground; and I imagine what the car tyres must look like, sunk in dirty water, and I also imagine us accelerating suddenly, surprising them, and the wheels, stuck for a few seconds in the mud, then splattering their eyes, faces, armour. Just as they were about to shoot, the car would emerge from the hollow and with a rasping noise we would head far away from them, bursting through the barrier and continuing on. I imagine that we weren't merely enduring history; we were also making it, and we wouldn't allow ourselves to be defeated by the invisible force of thick roots.

174

Boris raises his arms and places his hands on the nape of his neck. I follow suit. With those helmets covering their faces, I can't tell if the one who comes over to my side window is a man or a woman. They have blue eyes, and we stare at each other while they open the door – so gradually that the screech is like a bird chattering in my ear. Out of the corner of my eye I see that another one is doing the same to Boris's door. Fresh air runs through the passageway they've opened up and my mother's stench lifts. And I imagine that the men who had done that to Boris's parents were like this too: infinitely interchangeable, leathery beneath black chain mail. 'Where are you coming from?' 'From the mountains,' replies Boris without moving his hands from his nape. 'Where are you headed?' Where are we headed? Boris says: 'North,' and I turn my head and look at him, not understanding where his conviction comes from. And Boris opens the glove box and pulls out some papers with annotations and circles, and some maps with highways highlighted in phosphorescent colours. I see the various elevations, circles that grow wider and wider around a point; the blue colour of the rivers, the shadows in the mountainous zones, the green of the forests and the flat brownness of the desert. Some names were familiar to me, although I couldn't place them. They order Boris to get out of the car. They tell him: 'Come.' Five of the men lead him towards the old barracks beside the barrier; the other five stay to keep guard over me. And I feel something inside me gently tearing.

INFINITE

The border divided the plain itself. Like the hill divided the plain itself but its elevation crossed it and multiplied it. Like parents divide their children; and if you don't have siblings, they divide you. As you grow they chop you up into pieces, and then, when you're grown, you have to go around salvaging a loss that isn't yours. The only good thing about childhood is that it ends. There was also something that rose up between my parents, and with the years it got thicker and harder to get through. There were also the roofing sheets that separated the plots from the street. And the purple heartwood door of the neighbours' blue house, where some of us could read: 'You will never enter here.' And the rushing torrent that divided the field, where the cow splashed her hooves. The animals of the forest drank and bathed there but our dog was always afraid of the turbulent water and he'd watch it from a distance, with his ears pricked and his curled tail between his legs. For him, that was the end of the world. There was also the car and the loose time that separated Boris at the wheel from my dad at the wheel. And there was, of course, the space that opened up between his seat and my seat. There are also particles that aren't visible, like the deformed cells that separated Vita from her sister, but that together constructed a weird face that could be seen and a brain that worked differently from the rest. And what happened, the decisions that people took, also invisible, and that suddenly and forever separated those of us who stayed from those who fled.

SEA

What had happened in the barracks during those very long minutes; I didn't know how to ask him that. Nor did I know what to say to him about the maps and the notes and his very cold conviction. There was some sort of thin silence, and it seemed harmless, what could happen to us inside that car. A film separated the inside from the outside, as if my mother evinced a protective aura, and it widened into an impermeable sphere around us. And, with all that, there was the obvious assumption of my impotence and my expertise at remaining silent in the face of what I do not understand. Whispering when I should scream. It was as if all that were waves, one after the other, yes; but I was the whole entire ocean.

DREAMS

The barrier falls with a thud. We leave behind a border we did not know existed. On this side, the earth is arid and there is no vegetation: only dunes of gigantic boulders like pieces of bedrock randomly thrown. Through the rear-view mirror, the razor wire gradually grows smaller and, for the first time, we can see how long it is, extending into infinity and, as it does, rising even higher: it turns into extremely tall thick bars of rusted steel, like those trees. Once past the first enormous rock – it seemed to me as large as the hill by my home – dozens of people amass, like tangled ants re-organising their nest, in plastic shanties and awnings. From the fence we hadn't seen them. When they hear the engine scraping the metal, they stare at us suddenly: their eyes upon us. They look similar to each other, somehow. Linked by equal parts fatigue and illusion, the grubbiness of the dust mixed with skin toasted by the sun – scaling skin that clings, reptilian, to the desert. They run towards the highway and stand in front of the car. The smallest one is a boy with light eyes and a scar across his face.

don't forget that
the language I've always spoken to you in isn't mine
the language I'm writing to you in now isn't mine

my language is a different one
the big language, the one you call   _enemy_
I forgot it
I remember little
of the language they spoke to me when I was in my cradle
they stopped telling me 'not that word'
and instead told me 'what's   that word?'
we quickly forget where we come from
I was born, I left and I loved
I didn't know, then, that I was making a mistake
and the years have passed
the snow the sun more snow more sun

my son   don't ever forget a language
even though that language you speak isn't   mine
even though that language you speak doesn't want
mine
I made a son with a language that isn't mine

you know it,
we've seen it together
in the forest in the garden on these streets:

a fox a wolf a fish   dies just like   a man
a man dies just like another man
~~saying no to a language is saying no to a man~~
~~saying no to a man   is later saying no   to life~~

They ask us to get out of the car. From the border, the soldiers must have seen how they took us behind one of the rocks, to show us their tents. They must have heard, at a distance, the echo of the woman who told us that when the Lord created the world he had a few pieces left over and he tossed them here, that was why there are those cliffs and these immense bales in the middle of nowhere. Perhaps, if they'd been paying closer attention, they would have noticed how I breathe more shallowly when I see that crowd and their fragile homes and the way they tell us, all at once, that they've been waiting days, months and years to cross the border, that they've tried to several times: and some of them show us their stumps, with dignity and courage, and others show us their empty eye sockets, and the little boy strokes his scar with his hand. And, very softly, my heartbeat, again: discovering that they speak my little, shattered language, so far from home; not understanding how they've been able to survive, in a place where no one speaks it; where if they speak it they are no one.

SKY

There was the hovering question of whether it was possible to get angry with a dead person like my mother. Not be angry with them, get angry with them. Or suddenly be moved by a desire to tell them that they're wrong. Or call them a liar. Until then I had not discovered anything – over the course of the journey I only contemplated. And the sensations piled up on me like that, like waves. Just as the tide drags vestiges to the coast, there were also reminders: the men and women gathered at the border, and how their different bodies were similar, brought to mind the men with the shaved heads. And my mother. How with her man she'd recovered her language and I'm convinced they spoke it fluently, when I wasn't watching them; I imagine that when she made a mistake, he would correct her, smiling, stroking her hand, and she would find that pleasant and refined, and she would blush. And the sadness of a dead person is no longer sadness except for others – grief is a dart piercing the living. With those people, there, waiting for life behind a rock, I didn't give a shit about the language she'd raised me with or hidden to make me grow up. What matters to me, beyond how people die, is who has died and who is no longer speaking.

A woman. An old woman. She wants to go home – the place where she left her dog tied up on a very long leash so he could eat in the forest. A boy. For years he's been investigating where the back door to the Factory is and he wants to cross the border to go searching for it. Boris listens to him more attentively than to the rest. A man. With sunglasses, deathly skinny and with a shaved moustache. He's never been to the mountains or the surrounding area, he's always lived under the rule of law. He laughs every time he repeats 'the empire of law'. He says that he is fleeing the crimes he's committed and that, if he doesn't hurry, they'll catch up with him. A man. He earns his living collecting scrap metal. Now he looks for his missing daughter, who he thinks might be on the other side. A young man. White as a layer of cream. He says that getting across is his way of settling scores with his parents. A woman. With a handkerchief on her head like Vita's. She's convinced that she'll return, because she explains that there is an ancient law: even though it states that you cannot cross the razor wire fence, it says you can be buried there, on the other side. Sooner or later she will cross it, she repeats, even if she's dead. And yet another boy. With wide shoulders. He explains that they dig tunnels and underground passageways to get across the border. And I imagine the thick roots of the extremely tall trees that are in front of the fence. The indestructible lattice they must weave underground.

BORDER

An echo: my mother and I were linked by the same things that separated us. Maybe because we'd accumulated similar desires over the years, but also because later I discovered that it wasn't a coincidence, the shared hankerings, and that the inheritance had also consisted of opening her son's drawers and filling them with fears, and frustrations, and grief, but especially with desires, desires layered with impediments. Like the one we could've confessed once we were left alone, but we never did; that desire to have another name and love someone else, forever, and work no more than was strictly fair and necessary, and have a home with a dog waiting there, a vegetable plot, and wear out the roads with a fuming car – or motorcycle, it doesn't matter – and sleep beside the familiar warmth of someone else, and wake up with the familiar smell of that someone else, and concentrate all the sex in the world in a few minutes looking into the eyes of the drooling animal; and then go out and look up at the sky, and look down at the earth, and smile at the horizon like someone who knows they've done what they had to do. Take this delicate love out for a walk, and show it off on the streets of a city that's not too big or too small, and exchange smiles with acquaintances and compassionate looks with strangers; and go back home and end the night with one last fuck, while night flattens the landscape. But the thing is that between desire and reality, there is hysteria curled up, hidden, and you have to know how to control it so your body doesn't become uninhabitable. It was lucky, in fact, that we didn't verbalise our desire, because it was a secret that couldn't be spoken. And if we had spoken it, it would have disgusted us, almost as if we desired each other.

When we return to the car, and start the engine, they wave goodbye to us: moving their arms in an improbable choreography.

OBLIVION

I'd told Boris to close his eyes and imagine the life he wanted, if he could be the one to decide. I'd told him, when we passed under the ceiling of trees: 'Don't close your eyes, you're driving, but think about it as if they were closed.' He pretended to shut them, squinting until a line of white separated the lids. He didn't speak. Later he told me: 'Nothing's coming to me.' I suppose that he could only imagine some details, like me: that my mother was there, that I could go back home at any time, that this, the two of us being together, never ended. And not much more than that. I tried it too. I squeezed my eyelids tightly, focusing on the strength in my temples as my neck grew taut: I couldn't imagine anything. I had no idea what world I wanted, and I found it impossible to answer the question. All I had was that mantra we used to say to each other at the start but that we'd stopped saying, at some vague point along the way. It was something about being near the sea, buying a stretch of land and digging a vegetable plot, and having animals. Being able to swim in the sea and letting the movement of the air dry us off.

We stop the car when the sky blackens, at a turn in the highway that allows for a gentle inlet, hidden among some brambles. When he brakes, we hear the flowing of a river moving furiously. It sounds like an open faucet. Boris lowers the window and sticks his feet out, leaning his head on the seat's padding. I move to the back to deal with my mother. When I pick her up by her torso, I can't help searching for her heartbeat with my fingers: her body falls apart in my hands as if I were stirring the hill's damp earth. Silky. It's hard for me to recognise her lying there. I'm reminded of the weeks after my dad died, which she'd spent holed up in bed. I would bring her food and, since she didn't want to see me, I would leave it by her door. Hours later, I would come back for the tray, do the washing up, and put the plate back there full, at night. After a few months I ceased to exist, for her. Later, I occupied a new place in the house's order: I embodied his absence, I took his position, because now I was the one sustaining her. And I gave myself over to what I couldn't understand: what hurt me the most was not being able to detach from her, because a mix of guilt and love kept me moored to her. Loving my enemy: like now, when throwing her into the river seems crazy, but beyond her body, my mother is now an impediment.

We go down to the river. It gleams like the back of a salamander. The part closest to us is rushing, but further away it is more tame and there is a tranquil, almost still area. We take off our clothes. I find a new tightness in Boris's body, his flesh more glued to his bones; the days of our journey have emptied him out – how long has it been since we left home behind? – and his arms are longer, he is now spent, without the strength he gripped the steering wheel with on the first day. The water is freezing. He dives in quickly. I move slowly, trying not to lose my balance on the slippery rocks. When the water covers me and I am able to move my arms and legs, and get inside the river, I feel miraculously agile. There is no current. I grab Boris, who is trying to stay still, not swimming. He lets me touch him: the water calms him. My hands slip over some parts of his body, and on other parts it's hard to make them slide because the water leaves a rough film between us. We sink beneath the surface. Below, the protection we don't have above, where the more common happiness does not include us and our language is a goad like the beak on those birds who steal the eggs of another mother and eat the babies before they're born. In the water, I hear a singular silence. And, there beneath, the balance that Boris and I have achieved extends, less fragile, less provisional. Later, we enter a dreamless sleep – sometimes it seems that we sleep so time will move more quickly, the years passing between the eyeball and the lid. And Boris, like that, with his eyes closed and his cheek melting against the glass, seems to me, for the first time, disarmed.

BALANCE

SACRIFICE

Dragging her body didn't make me feel anything. I could hold it in my hands as if it were the body of a dead cat, a hoarse dirty kitten, with rigid arms straight as columns: I would walk, carrying it without halting, along the highway and through the mud, and wherever I had to walk. I would feel as though it were easy. I would feel a deep relief, a lightness, the order in the rain, trees and the night all breathing at once. What's happening is good, I would remind myself. There would be no accidental bonds, she wouldn't be alone either: my dad in his place, my granddad in his place, her in her place. The silty path at home, the hill, the wolves, the sky, the garden. In their place. And the cat in my arms. Everything would depend on me, and at the same time I would depend on all the rest. Nothing would worry me, and I would go everywhere with the body of the little animal hanging, splattered with mud, warming and chilling my chest. Like an offering.

When we get up, my legs feel strong and the skin covering my arms different, but my back hurts from sleeping in the car. Before continuing, I go to cover my mother, shield her face. My granddad always used to say, when a pig or a hen was born, that being born is like picking a flower, because as soon as you pluck it it's already dying, even though it seems full of life. What he didn't say is how unwieldy the flower is, when it's dead, and how, after withering, it quickly rots until it becomes fertiliser. Loving, on the other hand, he would recite, was contemplating the flower without picking it, not pulling it out by its roots: looking and entering without touching. But what did he know about flowers, he who had spent half his life thinking he was a hindrance. I, at that time, didn't see the rivers of ants carrying aphids that went up and down the stalks as if they were avenues, and left them in the buds and in the tenderest sprouts; and the aphids sucked their blood, and the few flowers that opened, opened up already wilted, even though they were alive; the ants kept going up and down, and when the tiny insects were brimming with sap, they took them down the branch so they could eat them all juicy with nectar in their tunnels. I look at my mother's eyes, and I cover her face.

Despite everything, I repeat to myself: 'Mistakes are the gateway to discovery.' And I know that it's not true, when from the passenger seat I look at Boris to ask him to turn around so we can go back home; but I don't say it, and he keeps his hand on the gear shift, without moving it, as if something were bothering him, his being so still and mute a sign of impatience, despite knowing that there is some word I've decided to keep quiet. I remember the man with the shaved head, every once in a while: the impression he left. As if he had always been aware and confident that, sooner or later, he would win. I enter his gaze, of that morning now so long ago, and I observe, through his eyes, the forest in a new way, as if from one moment to the next he'd understood everything. Moving forward is also always an abandonment. I look at Boris, he cracks the bones in his neck by turning it from one side to the other. And he keeps driving.

Another tunnel. So long that we don't know what time it is when we emerge: whether this orange light that is multiplying on the gleaming chassis is the sunset or the arrival of a new day.

SILENCE

'Do you still think this highway has no end? That the world is immense? That when we burned the house down we didn't affect the ones next to it, and the forest and the animals? That we can continue on like this, beside each other, moving forward, admiring the landscape and our absurd company? That it still isn't the time for each of us to return to the place we've always occupied? For each of us to relearn everything we've forgotten by the other's side? Do you still think I can't imagine what it would be like to live without this devotion, without this

It's a campground like the ones we'd seen in the photographs, when at school they would tell us: 'This is a campground,' and they would show us an illustration, so we would get the idea. Like when they told us: 'This is a hospital,' 'This is a mid-size city,' 'This is a skyscraper.' 'This is a campground.' And when a kid blurted it out in the other language, the one that wasn't ours, the teacher told him no with distant eyes, that that word didn't mean anything and that he had to erase it from his head, rubbing her hands on his forehead in front of the other kids. But the wooden sign at the entrance had a carved drawing of a fish with long whiskers and a wide tail, and beneath the word CAMPGROUND was written, in the same clumsy letters, FISH FARM. We enter, now pushing the car, and take the middle road. There are no plots, or bushes separating them, or any hut that looks like a reception area. We leave the car beneath the shadow of a tree. A hot wind drags, moving its heat everywhere, and lifting the dust from the ground; the sand scrapes my throat and a dirty feeling clings to my legs. From where we stop, you can see a couple of old yellowed caravans, and a tent with so many plastic sheets surrounding it that, even from a distance, it's clear that someone has lived there for years.

SYNONYMS

On the highway we'd seen a sign with the words FOOD and LODGING, and a straight arrow indicating the direction. Between the two words, the outline of a fish. Those simple words, we understood them. We could understand quite a few words, without them coming together into a sentence. And when we heard the language spoken, it sounded strangely familiar: maybe that was why it hurt us even more, because the ancient roots tied us together, whether we wanted them to or not, and meant, in the most essential and primitive way, that we couldn't not help each other. And the pain was doubled. We ignored the sign and kept on going, until the light covered us once again. The intermittent landscape changed so abruptly that we couldn't get used to certain trees, a particular terrain or a colour of the sky: they were also the hours, and our way of putting kilometres and kilometres behind us without getting out of the car, and recognising from the window another world, with different rules.

EXIT

Just as the car stopped rolling, the tired expression on Boris's face might have been what showed me that neither our direction nor our journey were shared, despite being beside one another. Where did that urgency come from? Where, that constant feeling that we were always late and everything was an obstacle to advancing as he would've liked? At the same time, it bothered me that he experienced my way of getting closer to him as a tether to keep him from leaving. And that wasn't it. But it was later, no doubt about it, it was later when he said it to me in the clearest way that Boris had of speaking to me. We had just crossed the darkness of the incredibly long tunnel and were readjusting to the light. We heard the sound of a final exhale – a bit deeper and longer than normal breathing – and the car gradually slowed down, halted; and I, a little happier, thought Boris had calmed down, finally.

At the campground, the dust filters an ancient yellow col-our over the surroundings. On the right-hand side, where we leave the car, there are some enormous fibreglass struc-tures. The way the dust moves above them, more slowly and lured inside, I figure they are filled with water. Fleeting blotches appear on their translucent walls – the beating of darkness. You can hear thumping, like a tenderiser hitting a piece of veal.

CAVE

It was then, no doubt about it, it was then, when we had to push the car up the highway, in the moment when I slipped and fell to the ground, and a bit of my knee was left amid the gravel of the detached asphalt; it was then that the membrane – plastic and incredibly thin like a blister – that separates love from revenge broke. Boris wore an animal face, like my dad's on some mornings, and while I was curled up in pain, he was shouting about why I couldn't for once and for all understand why he'd left home. 'It's not for you, it's for my parents!' And that slowness was killing him, inside and out. We pushed the car in silence. Silence: his punishment. And the harshness in his gaze, like the men who gathered fruit. Meanwhile, I wondered if Boris, in anger, had said things he didn't mean, or whether he had said truths that he wouldn't have said otherwise. Blood streamed from my knee. My knees grew weak. I could no longer find again the strength of agile arms or the freshness of cold water pricking my muscles. It was the sun, and the heat, and also the keen pain that any person feels when they are beside someone they love but can't speak to them, in that moment in which, suddenly, the other person becomes a stranger. A threat.

a man takes the place of another man
  someone will take my place
  someone will eat at the table
  someone will use my used sheets
  someone will yank on the doors the knobs the windows
  someone will occupy this house
to get rid of it, to inhabit it, to destroy it

I met your father: an idea
we made a home   this one
I was fleeing the others, my people
he was fleeing himself
fleeing   a verb that doesn't end
we found each other   we made a home
and then   a son
he opened his mouth and couldn't   speak
he looked you in the eyes and couldn't   speak

from top to bottom, my entire belly
the scar of a language   mine
two losses and a trace
you and   my language
in front of the mirror   my hand beneath my clothes

those who speak your language can hurt you
those who speak your language can want to hurt you
don't ever forget a language

204

because each language covers your back
in a different way
but every language is also a knife blade
on your throat
and no scars are left on necks   just the cut
the pouring blood

there will always be someone who will come after us
there will always be a man to take the place of another man
when he arrives, make sure that he can't use anything
that all that's left is charred ruins
and a dry garden
things belong to those who make them live

It's not like we have any tent to set up. Since we have to stop, we use it as a chance to shower, have a hot meal, stretch our legs and rest in the shade. We leave all the car doors open so it can air out. While Boris stretches out a plastic tarp on the ground and unloads our things onto it, I uncover my mother. It isn't her any more, sucked into her organs, with a mass of disappearing matter; she has aged and she has Granddad's face now. I cover her up again. From a distance a conversation in deep voices can be heard. I approach the bluish fibreglass tanks and, the closer I get, the harder and duller the banging sounds. Drops of water splatter my face and send the dust streaming down my cheeks. Since the thick walls are as high as my chest, I can rest my hands on the edge and look inside: massive fish that don't stop moving; slimy scales brushing, with barely enough space to change places. Many of them flap their tails above the water's surface, or a fin, struggling to breathe, or to be able to slide past amid the slippery backs of their brothers and move their bodies, dig a bit deeper, slightly change their fleshy perspective on the others.

OTHERS

From the fish pools, the conversation is louder. I walk over to it. From behind a tree, I see a group of men and women in a circle. Some of the men have darker skin, but the women are pale, with that kind of flesh that burns quickly in the sun. They shout. I can understand some of what they say, because some of them use my language, or both at the same time, taking words from one or the other indiscriminately. The mixture makes me laugh, as if there were interference inside their heads and the words emerged from their mouths without them chewing them over first. Also because of the empty bottles that are piling up beside the fire. Also, maybe, because of the isolation in that solitary place. That used to happen to me, too, before, when I hadn't seen new faces in a long time, that I would speak louder to those around me. One of them they call 'Lil Cuppa'. They say: 'Lil Cuppa, this,' and 'Lil Cuppa, that.' They must call him that for his cinnamon-coloured skin; and because he's small.

CHILDHOOD

I went up through the pathway between the two largest tanks. On either side were the stretched rectangles filled with water. In the ones on the left, there were small, long black splotches that moved nervously in circles. I dipped my hand in and pulled some out: they were tiny little fish, they must have been born just hours earlier, and they squirmed and baulked – as if how they moved on top of each other was written in their genetic code. On one side of their backs hung a thin little bag. I thought it must've been a placenta that nourished them while their mouths were still so small. Their eyes, two black spots. They moved their tails so quickly that you couldn't see the motion, just glimpse a shadow slipping from one side to the other.

Lil Cuppa gets up to take a leak and chooses the tree I am hiding behind: he pisses on my feet and, kneeling there, I see his closed eyes and his hands shaking his small reddish member. He opens his eyes and finds me there, with a rapt expression, regretting that I'd followed the sounds. Lil Cuppa, with a voice somewhere between stupid and friendly, surprisingly high-pitched, invites me to join them. I accept without much hesitation, because that combination of seated people had caught my eye: like small animals in a cave, they welcome me. And I am grateful to again be able to share time with other humans who are alive and who speak.

ADOLESCENCE

The fish in the two tanks further down were larger: only one could fit in my hand. They had big eyes and were grey with black stripes on their backs. All eyes. When they half opened their gill covers, I saw the empty gills chafing their bodies, and it turned my stomach, that slit opening and closing, cartilaginous. They respected the distances between them, not touching. And they moved at the same time, like a flock of birds: up and down, and then plunging; they swam quickly to the far end of the drum and, when one touched the wall, it turned, and the rest turned with it. Some had little curled brown strings coming out of them, which they paraded around like a tail for a while, until they detached and continued floating on the surface of the water. One of the fish was still little and had its bag stuck to its chest. When I tried to grab the little fish in my hands, one of the big ones ate it.

They pick the fish bones clean and toss them into the fire. They pile up the heads and tails on a plate. The conversation is led by a large man with elongated limbs. When he speaks, saliva gathers grittily in the corners of his lips and he sprays a scummy yellow spittle on those close to him. He, of course, doesn't realise it. And just watching him I sense his deceitfulness, scum in the corners of his mouth. The moon reflected in his rotted teeth. He comments on what the others say, making a final note that ends the discussion of one subject and sparks a new one; meanwhile he hasn't stopped stroking the thigh of the woman beside him. He repeats her name with his gluey mouth and she lets him cover her with wild trout kisses. They offer me fish and I eat so I'm full, for it's better to not be able to sleep from indigestion than from hunger.

MATURITY

In the tanks near the entrance, facing where we left the car, there were enormous fish. Monstrous. They had the eyes of the dead and their whiskers were thick antennae that extended to the depths of the open drums. Their backs screeched when they rubbed past each other, damp. With their tails they splashed water out, gradually emptying the reservoirs, condemning themselves to an even narrower and more crowded life. I threw a rock at them. Then, as if I'd punctured the bottom and the earth was sucking up the liquid, the water swirled as the fish launched themselves towards a single central point. They were hypnotic, pure flesh. Like aquatic bulls. With those big blind eyes that took up half their faces, and their muscular tails. They crashed against the walls, protesting. But also without any sort of pain. Then, the spiral dissolved and they brought their heads up to the surface, opening their mouths and begging the air for food: each mouth opened a grotto. And I was afraid to look at them.

They dance around the fire, singing, banging the empty bottles, the men touching the women, the women letting the men touch them, and I sit watching. Living has to be something more than this, I think. The flames illuminate the men's sunken faces, the women's pale faces, and dry the saliva of the tallest one, turning it into a scab. Lil Cuppa smokes and smokes some sort of thick cigarette that smells odd. He also chews some green plant stems that he moves around with his tongue. The men laugh as his face warps, dissolving into lilac tones, and his eyes light up the colour of blood. Later, he throws up as if pouring out all the water in the fish farm from inside his mouth. The very tall man looks at me and says: 'Tomorrow we'll take you to harvest some of the plants.'

GOLD

The very tall man and Lil Cuppa came to pick me up from where we were in our car. Boris, when we woke up, told me he wasn't coming. He pulled the papers and underlined maps out of the glove box, and stretched out on top of the plastic tarp on the ground. I asked him: 'What are you doing?' and he replied: 'Nothing.' That belittling tone, that irritating superiority in his words. Lil Cuppa, since he'd worked repairing trucks on the border, took a look at our car: the engine had surrendered. He could help us turn it into a house, if we wanted. I followed them outside the fence, where their car was parked. The tall man drove with one hand. With the other, he lit one cigarette after the other. I watched him in the rear-view mirror: he would stick them into the slit he had in his lip, a hole that, before birth, had sewn his mouth to his nose, and then he exhaled the smoke through his nostrils, without touching the cigarette. Like the hole that opened up in the mouths of the largest fish.

FORMULA

I had the feeling we were going backwards, retracing the road that Boris and I had marked out. We headed back towards the desert, to a dryness I couldn't stand and that, the first time, had seemed endless. I gripped the door handle because he drove fast and the car had no seat belts. He parked in the middle of the highway. The very tall man didn't lock it. Then they started to explain to me how it worked. They told me: 'You don't find it, it finds you.' They repeated: 'Don't look for it, it will appear to you.' And we walked. Time disappeared. The air burned so hot that I felt I was melting and getting lost in the sand. Maybe an hour had passed, or two hours, or three hours, and Lil Cuppa shouted: 'I found one,' and he lifted it up in his hands like a trophy. The tall man stopped, looked at him and kept walking. At some point I thought of Boris: I recited to myself that I had to trust that it would never end, and that what was to come had only just begun. I repeated: 'There is something of him in me, not a memory, a real presence that will not die.' Then, I thought the same thing about my mother. And I saw them there, too, walking with me, sweaty like me, covered up, wandering in search of one of those succulent plants.

The return trip is slow and fast at the same time. The hours melt over me. We wait for it to get dark, after the whole day in the sun, sucking and sucking on the bits still between my teeth. I try to make it last longer by searching for them in my mouth, patiently, and squeezing them against my palate with my tongue to extend the effect a little more, please, just a little more. I see my dad and my mother together, holding hands. The night opens up, and we lie on the ground, looking at the sky. Boris comes and shows me the maps and explains that we must follow the phosphorescent highway to reach our destination, with the rabbits, and with the plants, and with the sea water. The very tall man says: 'Let's go back.' My granddad comes too, like hail in the desert. We wordlessly follow the very tall man. Vita comes, with the animals, and the other old ladies, singing. And her sister with the weird expression. The cold makes me shiver. I can't feel my body and it walks alone, without my direction. It just walks. Me and his brother come, and they have soft, silky hands, with no scars. My desires have grown, inflated, and when they are closer than ever, they become memories, memories that slip away like drops after the rain, and I see them leave: my parents, Boris, my granddad, Vita, Me and his brother. There are some thoughts, though, that aren't soothed. Lil Cuppa tells me that it could last more than a day and that it would gradually get less and less. Sleep, eat and drink lots of water. In the car, my dad's voice still repeats that I must control my vices and the gates through which fruitless desire enters. We reach the campground just as the howling starts from the first beasts heading out to hunt at night.

FACE

I found it. I mean, it found me. It was huge. I told them: 'I found it!' Lil Cuppa came over, and looked at it, and his eyes lit up, and he told me it was a treasure, a gold mine, he told me that it was a well, an oil well, filled with money and life. He jumped and shouted, repeating: 'A gold mine, a gold mine!' I was happy and I didn't understand why. But Lil Cuppa hugged me, and murmured in my ear: 'A gold mine, a gold mine!' He offered me a slice; I had to chew it hard and hold the paste under my tongue. Sit and wait.

We say goodbye: they go down to the bonfire they light every night, and I head to the car. We don't know each other's names, because we assume each other's lives without having to ask. One of those peripheral relationships that only serves to kill time, and over time kills your life, because it makes your loneliness and frustration grow even more. The dappled night, splattered with milky stars. The campground doesn't have the desert's dry cold, which had swooped down from the sky and frozen the ground, and the succulent plants, and our bodies, stretched out there. In fact, there's a pleasant breeze and, in the distance, the tanks of water glitter, and it's lovely, because it's as if I were again approaching the Factory as it lit up in the early dawn, with a light from inside, as if it had swallowed a glow-worm and projected a brilliant beam from its open mouth. In front of the tanks, all you can see is the outline of the car. I thought that the chill of the temperature would make my mother happy, but later I realise maybe not. Heating up and cooling off must be like turning over the rotting flesh.

I open the back door to see my mother's body. The lump looks like a bunch of dry hay covered with a blanket, and a strong toasted aroma thickens in the air. She's reached the point where the waiting no longer matters, and I'm fine with having her there for another day, or two, or three. From the rigidity and coldness at Vita's house, to this expression now, shrunken and wrinkling into herself, and with fungus growing around her lips and eyes, and the dark murky colour of her face, the skin dry and at the same time damp, devoured by bacteria. I close the door. Boris must be sleeping up front or outside, on the plastic tarp. The coolness feels better and better. I hear the shouts of the men and the silence of the women. And the light that emerges from the plastic walls of the drums, stronger. I open the door again. I grab my mother by the shoulders, squeezing her hands against her belly. Her flesh doesn't seem like flesh, the way that it yields like sand. Then, I lay my hands flat under her back, so I have a better grip on her. That way, I can slide her over the mats and, little by little, I rest her on my knees and lay her out on the ground. I close the door.

before I arrived I wanted   it all
by the time I arrived I wanted   NOTHING
then how can you feel that you're alive?

I joined the party to fight the good
fight   it's a never-ending verb
then I forgot about the party for another life   leaving
and people don't forgive   abandonment

I forgot my name
I loved some men without knowing my name
I asserted some things without knowing my name
without knowing   their names
and one day, I abandoned them
but you can't abandon them   not them

people don't forgive you being someone else in front of them
leaving
I didn't choose to go   I left
— it's not the same thing
to stop repeating dead words   to flee

your father   before the forest
both of you   like a scar
I met your father
I followed him like a bull to slaughter
I forgot about myself again

222

can you forget the same thing twice, three times,
four times, five times?
he forgot   in other ways
he only sometimes spoke about the country,
about the language
I never told him where I came from   he never asked
but he   always knew ????   Yes YES

we didn't talk about it: I learned what I had to learn
and at the foot of the hill we made   a life
a home   a vegetable plot   a son
fear: would they come looking for me??
there was always suspicion   silence
hesitation: would they find me?
there was always suspicion   silence
if you have to go back to the past you can no longer choose
freedom   what?

you learn how to nurture
when you have a naked body in front of you   not before
first: your father
second: you
third: the scar   my hand beneath my clothes   the bark
meanwhile all the words I'd forgotten there upon me
like autumn leaves waiting to fall from the tree
and the new words to learn, those too   daggers upon me
sharp   dry??   blades

taking care of a body   your father   lost in himself
I searching inside him where was he
meanwhile: the leaves   the unsaid words
the words not   learned

then you   in my hands   that's it? why isn't he crying?
cry cry cry! cry!!
in the background: the forest, the house   silence
just a few glances   aimed at me
if I spoke with strangers they would tell me
'hush, you speak too much like them'
they recognised the accent
the unique way I pronounced words
the confusion always on my lips   the shame: not knowing
and they pointed with their fingers beyond the mountains
they told me 'hide that hellish accent'
and I   MORE silence   silence
I again learned how to watch pretending I was listening
REMEMBERING
in silence   I would hide behind the words I didn't say
I learned what I had to learn:
words, phrases, paragraphs, ideas   I repeated them   silence
continuing to learn to forget   forgetting
— you can never learn it well enough

the years have passed like flakes of dust dragged by the wind
passing   it's a never-ending verb
your father died and suddenly the fear   gone
no fear no doubt   no questions

but fear isn't there for a reason   it's just there
always, and it comes back   living with fear   learning
my world had ended long ago   when??
your father died and suddenly a silence that wasn't ME
where'd it come from? when had that world   ended??
the silence   NOW noise
from the factory nothing, that place was real   hell

224

later, all that happened
the light   the smell   the holes   the trucks
it was like I no longer was afraid, not ME
leaving again nope
things end when you say   enough
the empty city, the empty houses, the empty forest
then more noise than ever   and you   still
the scar that was fading   you
the mixed-up words: the old ones reappear
they die   the new ones   going back to the cradle: never
speaking that language again
the one they used to say NO to you for the first time
speaking again   hope??
but always   hope's the first thing you have to lose
just in case: don't wait up for hope

the empty forest, the empty houses, the empty city
who would come find me in that forest?
who would now tell me NO in a language
without a language?
later the tanks left
later you left

my son, the fire is always inside: like napalm in the heart

goodbye

When I try to drag her by the hands, I hear the sound of bones detaching from cartilage and her joints loosening. But no. No, no, no. I tell myself: 'Stop.' I am afraid I'll rip her arms off. And she has to stay in one piece, yes. I go to the other side of the car and grab the tarp. Boris isn't there; he must be asleep in the front seat. I push her onto the tarp by rolling her like a log and folding her into a bundle. And that day, when I was convinced she was goading me, as we stood over Granddad, and she told me to chop him into bits and bury him in the garden. When years earlier she had bust open the pig's head with the shovel and left it dead flat. The strength she drew from her bony body, now gathered in plastic wrapping. I grab it by one end and, walking it backwards, I drag it to the tanks. I hug her again from behind and pull her up into the passage that extends between the two blocks of water. She weighs less dead. And then I climb up.

BED

The cold felt cold until my blood grew even colder and I slept. On the dust, beneath the tree, with the gleam of the fish tanks lighting up the night. My mother inside. Thinking that I was headed towards some fate, without knowing it, felt like the assumption of a rich child. Maybe what felt to me like fate was actually the belief of someone who is more than just the sum of the hurt they've caused. Someone who, against all odds, is also the strength found in hiding from violence and staring at it through the half-open door, and of being the bitter gulp of steeped scrubweed when there's no fennel, or passion flower, or rosemary. And I fell asleep in that night that wasn't yet fully night.

I unwrap the body. One corner of the plastic tarp falls into the water and the fish immediately rush over. One of the largest arrives first and nibbles on her, leaping with its tail above the surface of the water. I have to pull it out, quickly, because it was yanking and carrying her away. I didn't know how to let her go. I was ashamed to say goodbye knowing that I wasn't doing what she'd asked of me, which, from the start, I'd understood as a promise: to bury her far from home. I wasn't exactly breaking my promise. I still blamed her for something I couldn't name, not because I was hiding it, but because I didn't quite know what it was. I wanted to scream, loud. But that would wake up Boris and bring Lil Cuppa and his friends running over, and they wouldn't understand a thing, seeing me there, like that, dumping a body in with the fish. I roll her over a couple of times and she falls into the water. The carp come together like a stain. More and more of them come out from underneath. They grow. They multiply. The ones on the outer edge slither over the others' backs to get to the centre. I hear the sound of many mouths swallowing at the same time. The younger ones, in other tanks, ricochet, run through by an electric force. A minute later, the stain has dissipated, and the fish are again motionless in their narrow living space.

EDDY

There was something in all that that both transcended and contained me at the same time, that went through me and remained inside me, but that could also be spat out somewhere – who knows where, very far away, in a place I couldn't actually envision: how can I forgive myself? The simplicity of the question made me slack. It exhausted me and made me fall to the ground in a stupor. Boris. I was thinking, Boris. But it also ignited something in me, organs, blood and lymph glands in flames, and it wouldn't let me hide or move my brain to some other place. The question stunned me. Half dead and half alive at the same time. Like everyone. And like Boris: also half dead and also half alive. But I'm stronger than him, I thought. If I'd never felt fear, Boris, if I'd never felt it, I wouldn't have known that there is something stronger than the fear that is greater than me. 'Boris,' I was thinking, 'Boris.' Nor would I have remained waiting for this. For this, now. Here. Like this. No. Not now.

I wake up. The morning has bloomed, while I was stretched out waiting for something, for Boris to come out of the car and say let's go on. I couldn't remember the previous day, it withdrew from me, and I was unable to put together the bits and pieces and reconstruct them in a time-line. I get up and open the rear door. Why is my mother not there? I feel my legs rooted to the ground, like those of a large heavy animal. Then some bluish images come to me, of a sky blue, of a sea blue, of an electric blue, with artificial light that points at me with a torch from the depths of the water. The plastic comes to me. The putrefying flesh comes to me. The sound of gravel stirring and my arms dragging a weight comes to me. The fish come to me. The black hole and them leaping into it all at the same time comes to me. I remember. A dizziness rises up in my eyes, acidity travels up my throat, the eddy of greasy carp upsetting my stomach. I open the driver's-side door to wake up Boris. His seat is empty. Mine is too. I throw up, like Lil Cuppa the night before last, and, then, I feel better.

MAPS

It had been a journey downward, towards a centre we couldn't locate. As if the hill pointed to the earth's core instead of rising towards the heavens. We hadn't advanced alone, thousands of people had travelled with us, from such different and such distant places, with such different and such identical languages to ours, and who searched, at the same time, for the same kernel of meaning. In the depths, at some point, we'd discovered a water that healed us, but that also softened our fingertips and made us floppy, weak. In the deepest place, beyond the forest's undergrowth, beneath the moss, the earthworms, the damp soil, the rotted humus, the bedrock, the mines, the oil basins, the solid magma and the liquid magma, the condensed centre of the earth, I thought that there I would find a new way of loving: a page with instructions, with precise detailed steps, without mistakes, or failures, or unknown words. Leaving behind yesterday's world had been the easiest part. And amid so many dangers, there was still one thing left: me?

I go up to Lil Cuppa's camp. The women aren't there. The men are still sleeping, lying like beasts, curled up together. I wake him up. His eyes are filled with damp rheum. He wipes it away, stretching. I repeat: 'Come on, Lil Cuppa.' He gets up on his knees. 'Come on, Lil Cuppa!' I ask him: 'Do you know where Boris is?' 'Who's Boris?' I try again: 'Have you seen a guy leaving here, from our car, leaving the campgrounds?' I search everywhere for him, in the toilets, the showers, everywhere. I go back to the tanks where the fish float calmly. To the entrance. 'Boris,' I think, 'Boris.' All I see are three parked cars and the start of the highway, opening up onto the desert. There is nothing below either. My legs hurt, my arms. I imagine Boris as a black spot illuminating the gilded landscape. A spot becoming smaller and smaller on the line that separates the earth from the sky. I try to think of the moment when I last saw him, but I couldn't remember, and I could only repeat that when you see someone for the last time you often don't know it'll be the last time. And then I remember: him, lying on the plastic tarp, with the maps and papers in his hands, turning them over and taking notes. I didn't understand it. I didn't know who to be angry with either. And I feel a pain burning my stomach, as if invisible claws, as if blades, as if my dad's small sharp jack knife were jabbing between my navel and my ribs, piercing me, eviscerating me and hiding inside my body.

232

UNDERSTANDING I

UNDERSTANDING II

UNDERSTANDING III

UNDERSTANDING IV

UNDERSTANDING V

What does love mean
what does it mean 'to survive'
A cable of blue fire ropes our bodies
burning together in the snow   We will not live
to settle for less   We have dreamed of this
all of our lives

ADRIENNE RICH